THE CALDER GAME

THE CALDER GAME

BY

BLUE BALLIETT

ILLUSTRATED BY

BRETT HELQUIST

SCHOLASTIC INC.
NEW YORK TORONTO LONDON AUCKLAND
SYDNEY MEXICO CITY NEW DELHI HONG KONG

This book was originally published in hardcover by Scholastic Press in 2008.

ISBN 978-0-439-85208-1

Text copyright © 2008 by Elizabeth Balliett Klein. ▲▲▲ Illustrations copyright © 2008 by Brett Helquist. ▲▲▲ All rights reserved. ▲▲▲ Published by Scholastic Inc. SCHOLASTIC, SCHOLASTIC PRESS, AFTER WORDS, and associated logos are trademarks and/or registered trademarks of Scholastic Inc. ▲▲▲ Photograph in the After Words section of Blenheim Palace, Woodstock, Oxfordshire, England, UK by Russel Kord / Alamy. Second photograph in the After Words section is an overhead aerial view of Marlborough hedge maze, Blenheim Palace, Oxfordshire, England, UK © by Skyscan Photolibrary / Alamy.

20 19 18 17   19 20/0

Printed in the U.S.A.   40

First Scholastic paperback printing, September 2009

The text type was set in Hoefler text.
The display type was set in
Metro LT Black LT Two and Trajan Pro.
Book design by Marijka Kostiw

To Bill:

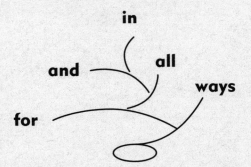

ACKNOWLEDGMENTS

▲ ▲ ▲ Writing a book is a balancing act, and love and thanks go to my family and friends. My husband Bill made several trips to Woodstock with me, remained calm in the midst of hedge mazes and British traffic circles, and took hundreds of Woodstock and Blenheim photographs. Our daughter Althea lived with the black cat that became Pummy in *The Calder Game,* and managed to capture and share him by e-mail. The real Pummy was always a help, in part by being so round and fierce; he reminded me that all things must keep moving.

For their vision and expertise, many thanks go to the team at Scholastic, in particular to my marvelous editor David Levithan, to Charisse Meloto and Marijka Kostiw, to Linda Biagi, and to Ellie Berger and Lisa Holton. For her wisdom and guidance, many hugs go to my agent Doe Coover, and of course to Amanda Lewis.

The Chicago Public Library has played a part in the making of this book. For their generous support, warm thanks go to Rhona Frazin and Mary Dempsey, and to Bob Sloane in the Art Information Center. Alexander Rower offered advice, information, and the unexpected joys of visiting the Calder Foundation. Ruth Horwich kindly shared both stories and art. Karen Wiseman and John Forster, at the Education Office at Blenheim Palace, have answered my questions with great patience and even sent me a not-for-everyone map. Many thanks to Jim Hecimovich for on-site explorations.

Alexander Calder's work has delighted me for as long as I can remember. This book is my way of thanking him.

I make what I see.

It's only the problem of seeing it.

— ALEXANDER CALDER

∧ ∧ ∧

Nobody ever listened to me

until they didn't know who I was.

— BANKSY

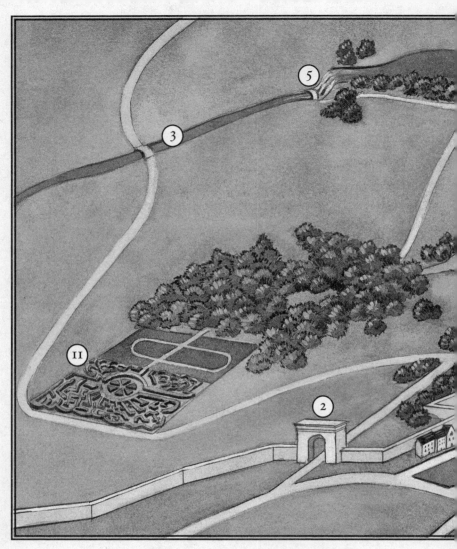

⋀ ⋀ ⋀ CALDER GAME MAP KEY

1	TRIUMPHAL ARCH	5	GRAND CASCADE
2	HENSINGTON GATE	6	ROSAMUND'S WELL
3	RIVER GLYME	7	TEMPLE OF DIANA
4	QUEEN POOL	8	VANBRUGH BRIDGE

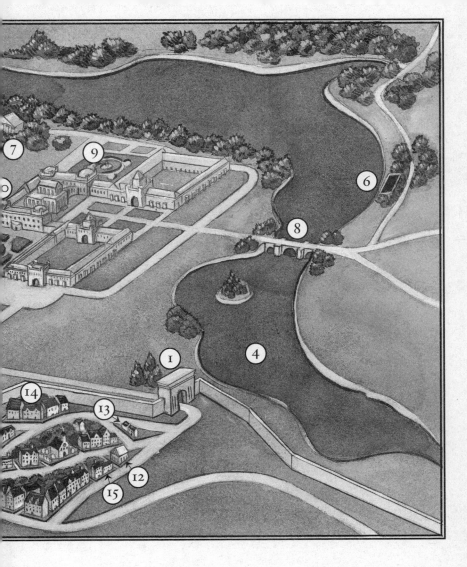

The setting is the start. The story hangs
from that hook, and the characters move
slowly around one another.

Each piece has its own shape and size.

The characters think they see
the wires that connect them.

But that isn't possible.

Or is it?

Who makes the rules?

CHAPTER ONE

▲ ▲ ▲ The setting is a very old town in England. It is dawn, a pale October dawn that pours through the streets like cream, erasing line and dissolving shadow. Red ivy stirs against damp stone; the houses are stone, the walls are stone, the street is stone. A lace curtain has escaped through an open window and waves unseen in the early light. Now a black cat blinks, stretches, and slowly crosses the empty square, stepping carefully around a raised sign that reads, MINOTAUR, ALEXANDER CALDER, 1959.

Someone sneezes behind closed shutters. A light goes on in a kitchen and a man in plaid pajamas fills a brass kettle. In other houses, butter sizzles and silverware clinks. The first truck of the day rattles across cobblestones and comes to a sudden stop. The driver sits for a moment looking straight ahead, his mouth open, then hops out and hurries to a nearby door. He bangs the knocker twice, sticks his head in, and shouts, "It's gone! The sculpture is gone!"

Soon enough, the town realizes that a boy is also gone.

CHAPTER TWO

▲ ▲ ▲ Exactly two weeks earlier, on a shiny, blue morning in the United States, three kids sat talking.

"Your dad is really taking you to England?" Petra Andalee asked, her voice thin with surprise.

Tommy Segovia's eyebrows shot up and his mouth opened in a slowly widening O. "Lucky," he muttered.

Calder Pillay pulled a piece of yellow plastic out of his pocket and ran the W-shape back and forth over one leg, back and forth between Petra and Tommy. "Yeah, I wish you guys could come," he said. "We're going next week, so I even get to miss school."

The three sat silently for a moment, banging their heels against the hollow sides of a circular piece of sculpture near the University of Chicago campus. Sun glinted off the metal, making it difficult to see.

Tommy, Calder, and Petra were all twelve, and all lived in the neighborhood known as Hyde Park, on the South Side of Chicago. Tommy and Calder had been friends since second grade, and Petra and Calder were much newer friends. Tommy and Petra weren't really friends at all, but they were trying; at times this threesome balanced perfectly, and at times it fell apart.

All were seventh graders at the University School, and all had a new classroom teacher they hated. At least they agreed about that. Her name was Bettina Button, and she never said what she meant. Even worse, she pretended she was always right. She had a flat face that fit her name and a tight helmet of hair the color of American cheese. Her clothes were pastel — pale greens and blues and pinks that might have been soft and gentle on someone else, but on Ms. Button looked more like battle gear. She ignored questions, looked busy when she wasn't, and had the kind of ungenerous smile that stopped the minute it wasn't needed. According to Ms. Button, learning was a job that left little time to experiment and no time to talk.

Their teacher from the year before, Isabel Hussey, had loved class investigations, understood noise and mess, and always listened. Her long, swishy hair was forever trying to escape from clips and ties, and sometimes she wore earrings that didn't match. She admired the colors red and black. No classroom idea was too odd, and no approach too unusual — forever curious, she was not afraid of making mistakes. In comparison to Ms. Hussey, Ms. Button was a disaster. No, she was more than that: She was deadly.

"You get a break from the Button," Tommy said wistfully.

Calder held the yellow W like a strange visor over one eye, cutting the glare. It was one of a set of twelve pentominoes that he carried everywhere, and Petra and Tommy were used to seeing him fiddle with them while he thought. Shaped like letters of the alphabet, the set was actually a math tool; Calder used it for playing around with number patterns, geometry, and his own puzzles.

He'd also discovered that the pieces worked beautifully for other kinds of problem-solving. In fact, he was convinced that pentominoes could do almost anything.

"My dad is going to a conference on city gardens in a place called Oxford, but we're staying in a small town nearby. Someone offered him this extra airline ticket, and he and my mom thought I should go. I guess there's lots for me to explore — even a real hedge maze made of symbols."

"Awesome," Tommy said. He thumped his backpack savagely, then picked his nose. "I wish we could escape, too."

Tommy lived alone with his mother and his pet goldfish, Goldman; they always had a cozy home, but had moved many times. They had even left Chicago the year before, which was a disaster. Tommy was very glad to be back, but still wouldn't have minded going on a trip like this, especially during the school year. He was an expert collector, and had picked up street treasures for as long as he could remember. He was sure that England, with all its old stuff, must be fabulous for finders.

Petra was busy fishing for a red sock that had disappeared in her shoe. "A maze with a message, she said. "You'll be around bushes that speak!"

Calder and Tommy nodded. They both knew the way words came alive for Petra. She always carried a pocket notebook, and believed that language was more than a string of symbols — it was a landscape, a place with its own secrets. Coming from a large, noisy family, she loved everything about writing: the privacy, the curves and lines of letters on a page, the quiet way an idea sometimes appeared out of nowhere.

She lifted her head and stopped tugging. "Hey, I wonder if the symbols can be understood while you're wandering around lost, inside the maze?"

Calder shrugged happily. "I'll find out."

Tommy groaned. "Yeah, *and* you get excused from any more ruined field trips," he said, giving Calder a whack.

"Ow! Just while I'm gone." Calder whacked him back.

Petra, retying her shoe, only sighed.

All thought back to a trip the week before to the downtown Museum of Contemporary Art. With Ms. Hussey, the trip would have been thrilling; with Ms. Button, it had been humiliating and frustrating, a day of tangled disappointments.

Although the three kids had no idea at the time, this field trip was the quiet start of a dangerous and extraordinary game, a game that circled around the wishes and dreams of someone they had never met.

CHAPTER THREE

ᐱ ᐱ ᐱ That September, Chicago had exploded with the largest-ever show of the artist Alexander Calder's mobiles. Pieces borrowed from collections around the world filled the entire Museum of Contemporary Art.

A mobile is a sculpture with parts that move; it has four dimensions, because it changes over time. When Calder first began making them, his invention shocked the art world. Sculpture that could change from one moment to the next? Was this possible, and was it still art? Suddenly, here was sculpture that was playful yet serious, simple in design yet rich in variation — people looked, and then looked some more. How had Calder done it?

The artist's changeable creations excited some of the greatest minds of the day. Jean-Paul Sartre, a famous French thinker, wrote in 1946:

> *A mobile, one might say, is a little private celebration . . . a pure play of movement. . . . There*

is more of the unpredictable about them than in any other human creation. No human brain, not even their creator's, could possibly foresee all the complex combinations of which they are capable. . . . If you miss it, you have lost it forever. . . .

He also compared a Calder mobile to a jazz improvisation, and to the flow of pattern seen in the sea.

Albert Einstein apparently sat and watched a Calder mobile for a very long time, so long that people wondered what he was doing. He muttered, with admiration, that he wished he had thought of it.

Calder created thousands of mobiles between 1930 and his death in 1976. Most consisted of a number of smooth metal disks connected with wire and painted black, white, red, yellow, or blue — only primary colors. The artist explained that the inspiration behind his earliest mobiles was the solar system: objects suspended, yet in motion. He also mentioned bubbles, snowflakes, coins, and poetry.

Never before had so many Calder mobiles been seen in one place. They ranged in size from palm-sized to several stories high. Written on the museum's walls, in red and black, were words spoken by the artist and others, as well as photographs of Calder in his studio and in his homes in France and Connecticut. For those in other countries who loved his art, it was a Calder feast, and an excuse to come to Chicago for a visit. Thanks to an anonymous donor, the museum opened its doors to everyone, free of charge, for the length of the exhibit.

▲ ▲ ▲ Tommy had not been enthusiastic about the field trip to see this show. As the class trooped off the school bus, he scowled.

"We have to wait in that LINE?" he asked, then muttered a bad word, but not softly enough. Ms. Button spun around.

"You'll not only wait in line, you'll wait at the very *end* of our class line," she said in a voice that sounded painfully like an overstretched rubber band. Tommy mimicked her silently, his eyes half closed, as he wandered slowly toward the back.

When Ms. Button saw the grins on other kids' faces, a crimson flush crept upward from the collar of her shirt. As she spun angrily away, an unexpected thing happened: A button popped off her coat. It flew, bounced, and rolled, spinning to a perfect stop by Tommy's sneaker. He picked it up.

He glanced quickly toward Ms. Button. She hadn't noticed.

The class watched, fascinated, as Tommy slid the large, baby-blue button into his pocket. No one said a word.

He took his place quietly — the class was near the end of a line that snaked around the block. Ms. Button had warned them before leaving school that there would be a wait outside on the street, and that she expected them all to stand in silence. She'd allowed each one of them to bring two dollars to buy a souvenir, but no clipboards or pencils. What would happen, she had asked, if someone accidentally drew on a piece of art? Remembering this, Tommy rolled his eyes, peering impatiently over the sea of heads. Ms. Hussey had *always* wanted them to bring something to write or draw on when they went to a museum. Now there wasn't even anything to do while they waited. Plus, he wasn't allowed to stand with either Calder or Petra. Ms. Button had separated all friends for the trip, hoping they would behave. *Behave* . . . that was her favorite word. Sometimes it felt like they were all being punished just for being kids.

Ms. Button was now patrolling back and forth in front of the class like an army general. Tommy waited until she turned away from him and then threw a pebble, hitting Calder on the ear. Calder scratched his head.

Tommy tried again. This time, his old friend looked around, raising his eyebrows in a silent question.

Tommy slowly inched the blue button into sight, holding it as if he were going to flip it like a quarter, and then slid it back into his pocket, timing it all so that Ms. Button wouldn't see. Calder grinned, but from where he was standing, he couldn't keep track of Ms. Button's every move. With a quick glance over his shoulder, he faced Tommy, held the F pentomino upright on the top of his head, and crossed his eyes.

Ms. Button swooped down on him. First she snapped her fingers, then she held her hand open in front of his face. "I'll take those. All of them. Right now, and you won't see them again for some time. What did I tell you about bringing toys on this trip?"

Calder's hand remained in his pants pocket, and no pentominoes appeared. "They're not toys," he said slowly.

"Oh, and I suppose a math tool is something you stick on the top of your head?" Her tone was biting.

Calder slowly pulled several pentominoes out of his pocket and handed them over.

Ms. Button snapped her fingers again, standing motionless until she had all twelve pieces.

Calder's shoulders drooped and he watched anxiously as Ms. Button threw his pentominoes carelessly into her shoulder bag. He knew she didn't value them. What if she lost one? That was his oldest set. Plus, he felt disgusted by the idea that they were in the same bag with her lipstick and tissues.

Worry and a gnawing sense of injustice now dulled his excitement about going to the museum. He'd hoped that something fabulous would happen to him on the day they went to visit the exhibit. But not anymore.

Calder Pillay had been named after the magical Alexander Calder. Long before their son was born, his parents had become fascinated with the artist's work — it was one of the things they loved about Chicago. There were three giant Calder sculptures in the city, public pieces that dated back to the 1970s.

The Pillays always went out of their way to walk beneath and through *Flamingo,* which rose some five stories high in a downtown plaza. A cheerful red creature, the sculpture swooped in a bridge-like arc between black skyscrapers.

Flying Dragon lived in the garden next to the Art Institute of Chicago. The Pillays thought it looked like a cross between a huge butterfly and an airplane.

And then there was the gigantic *Universe* in the lobby of the Sears Tower, one of the tallest buildings in the world. Calder's parents had taken him to visit this again and again — yellow, blue, red, and black, the separate motorized parts turned and spiraled around one another in countless combinations. Alexander Calder was clearly an extraordinary thinker, and Calder Pillay had grown up liking his name.

He'd seen many pictures of the artist's other work — wire circus figures, prints, rugs, brass jewelry, and even cooking utensils. He'd been taken to small exhibits of mobiles in Chicago, but had never seen more than five or six together.

These airy, drifting sculptures felt incredible, almost too perfect to believe: They always moved in a just-right way. Calder knew there were hundreds to see in this show, and had been so excited about going that he'd been up before his parents that morning. He was determined to have a terrific day despite Ms. Button.

After all, how could anyone get in the way of the great Alexander Calder?

CHAPTER FOUR

▲ ▲ ▲ Petra, watching from another part of the line, felt terrible for Calder and even Tommy. Why was it that the boys in the classroom got in trouble so much more than the girls? Ms. Button was always taking things away from them or making them sit by themselves.

Yesterday Tommy had been sent out of the room for saying to Ms. Button, "What's so great about this dead Calder guy, anyway?" Petra knew Tommy wasn't big on museum art, and was really asking. Ms. Button, however, seemed to think it was all a part of a plot.

"You kids are trying to sabotage this field trip, aren't you?" she asked when the class giggled. "Can't you take anything seriously?"

It made Petra feel sick. Ms. Button seemed to have no idea of how much they were capable of doing. She was too busy trying to maintain order, which of course made everyone try to be bad.

Sunk in their own vaguely sad thoughts, the kids shuffled toward the museum. And the quieter the class got, the more relaxed Ms. Button became. Didn't she understand that silence was sometimes a sign that things weren't going well?

The class dragged quietly up the long flight of stairs to the museum. At the top, Ms. Button forced them into a tight clump and reminded them grimly of all the rules: no touching, use polite voices, everyone must stay together. She said all this with her eyes hard and her forehead creased into a fence, the lines both vertical and horizontal. Tommy called it her tic-tac-toe head, only this time it didn't feel funny. If even one person misbehaved, Ms. Button warned, the entire class would lose recess for a week.

Once inside the building, though, something uncontrollable began to happen that even Ms. Button didn't have a punishment for: wonder.

The museum was filled with movement, and with irregular, delicate clangs and swooping zings. Hidden ceiling and wall fans provided just enough moving air, and subtle lighting added shadow. Flurries of bright color floated, danced, dove, and dipped, their shapes slipping

across walls, floors, fabric, skin, and questioning brains.

Calder's forms made Petra, Calder, and even Tommy think of other things: perhaps a stone, a leaf, a pear, a cookie with a bite out of it, a mask, a wing, a rudder. The pieces within each mobile moved unpredictably around one another, and, depending on where a person stood, everything could look different. Was there a pattern? Hard to say. With a little breeze, a disk could flatten into a line, a crescent moon could become a comma, a bird could vanish. Some of the sculptures rose from below, like elegant trees, and others hung overhead, changeable constellations that made it impossible not to stop and look up. Visitors of all ages moved quickly at first, and then more slowly, and then slower still. It became clear that a person could look forever and never discover everything there was to see.

A chorus of whispers rose from Ms. Button's class:

"I see a ballet slipper!"

"A boomerang!"

"A carved pumpkin!"

"A dog's nose!"

Tommy's mouth fell open in those first few minutes, and he forgot how little he liked museums and how much he hated Ms. Button. With sudden clarity, he saw each mobile as a finder's display, an amazing way to make a collection come alive. He pictured each of his own treasure piles — his bottle caps, his chopsticks and spoons, his stack of transit stubs — bobbing happily over his bed at home. An exhibit! Could he actually do it?

Calder forgot that his pentominoes weren't in his pocket, and tried to figure out how the artist had balanced all of the pieces *and* planned their movement when both the shapes and the weights were irregular. Each mobile was truly a complex puzzle: Had Alexander Calder experimented for hours, the way Calder Pillay did with his pentominoes?

Petra forgot the frustration of not being

allowed to write, and thought instead about pulling sentences apart and balancing words in three dimensions, as if they could float off a page. Words as things, not just meanings . . . words in space, words set free! Could it be done? Petra's mind felt as if it were exploding with possibilities.

The number of open mouths in the exhibit echoed the rounded shapes floating overhead and on all sides — an unexpected symmetry of forms that could only be caught if you happened to be watching the faces watching the art.

One adult was watching both faces and art, and this person noticed when Tommy bellowed, "Look, Calder, it's Goldman!"

He was pointing to a large, hanging fish outlined in wire and filled with small pieces of artfully suspended trash, fragments of broken glass, pottery, and machine parts that twinkled as they moved. The wall label read FISH, 1945.

Before this witness had time to wonder who Goldman was and why the boy was talking to Alexander Calder, a teacher hissed fiercely, "Is the word *silence* too difficult for you to under-stand?" as if the boy were the dumbest kid alive.

The witness's mouth fell open in yet another O-shape.

Petra heard also, and glanced in Tommy's direction. His eyes were now slits, a sure sign that he was under attack. They all were, Petra thought miserably, remembering Calder's drooping shoul-ders. She hoped Tommy never gave back Ms. Button's coat button. *Never.*

Without her writing tools, Petra concentrated on absorbing everything around her. She'd out-smart Ms. Button by soaking it all up and then recording it on the bus, where she'd tucked her notebook under a sweatshirt.

The mobiles felt like no other experience, Petra thought to herself, and seeing so many together was clearly — what? A gift. The *Time* magazine article in her pocket was right: This was generous art, and art that held everyone's attention. As she surreptitiously pulled out the article, wanting to read it again, she heard a little girl scream, "A flying cow!" and "A frog walking!" She then overheard a woman nearby marveling, "This isn't art, it's alive. It has a mind of its own!"

Petra turned to see a tall, red structure with three legs, a long neck, and a cascade of silvery leaves descending in a graceful arc from the tip of the neck — or was it a nose? The wall label read ALUMINUM LEAVES, RED POST, 1941. As Petra watched, one of the leaf shapes bobbed gently toward her, as if to say hello. She smiled at it, and gave a tiny, one-fingered wave.

She then ducked her head, reading:

An exhibit not to be missed, this show speaks to people of all income brackets, races, and ages. Shifting continuously, each of these mobiles weaves a spell, a long story that no one will ever witness again — not in exactly the same way. There are no rules here, no beginnings and no ends. Perhaps Calder's secret lies in the idea that each mobile is, truly, a metaphor for the experience of living, for the interconnected movement of separate elements that make up a life. Each mobile tells us to stop, to wonder, to wonder some more, and to celebrate. This is art that will surprise again and again.

Yes, Petra thought to herself just as she saw Ms. Button's skirt swishing in her direction. She stuffed the article back in her pants pocket, but her teacher was already snapping her fingers.

"It's mine," Petra said quietly, folding her hands in front of her. "And it's an article about this exhibit."

As Ms. Button glared at Petra, trying to figure out what to say, dots of sweat popped out on her upper lip. Tommy, despite himself, watched with interest. He hoped with all his heart that Petra would win.

Just then, Ms. Hussey flew around the corner with her new group of sixth graders. She was laughing, and everyone talked in excited voices, their faces bright with expectation. Each kid had his or her own clipboard and pencil, and suddenly Petra wanted to cry. Ms. Button turned stiffly away, as if she knew she'd gone too far.

Petra wondered how her new teacher could be so unaffected by this artist's feeling of joy, his *here-it-is-take-what-you-want* spirit.

As Petra hoped and prayed that even a pinch of Alexander Calder's magic would rub off on Ms. Bettina Button, the seventh graders were forced to walk, in unnatural silence, past one amazing sight after another. Unable to share with Calder or even Tommy, Petra stared. She noticed that young kids who had been led into the show looking bored — kids who had stood near them in the line — were now skipping ahead, dragging the adults who had brought them. She saw old people who had stumped into the museum in a grumpy way now looking complete, at peace, almost weightless themselves.

What was going on? It was hard, logically, to understand. But then, so was Calder's art. Simple? Only at first glance. Complex? Clearly, the answer should be yes. This is art that changes people, Petra thought to herself, people of all ages. But how?

Perhaps Alexander Calder's mobiles are working miracles, she thought. *Miracles!* It was a perfect word here, smooth and burbly and somehow floating. Thinking of her friend Calder and how he always shuffled things around, she let the letters in the word *miracles* drift and resettle in her mind. She found *rise*, then *miles*, then *clear*, then *risc*. Calder Pillay was never big on spelling — he'd think of *risk*.

Risk . . . Where was Calder, anyway?

CHAPTER FIVE

▲ ▲ ▲ Exhausted by trying to control her class, Ms. Button forgot to count them until they'd been inside the show for almost forty minutes.

"WHO is missing?" she asked the group, too flustered to figure it out.

At first there was no response, but the group looked perkier. Who had run away?

"Maybe he's in the bathroom," Tommy said at last.

"WHO?" Ms. Button said, now embarrassed but still clueless.

"When you gotta go, you gotta go," Tommy added. Petra grinned. There was a ripple of giggles.

The class, in unspoken agreement, didn't tell: Ms. Button took a full five minutes to figure it out.

▲ ▲ ▲ A large room at the Museum of Contemporary Art had a sign outside the door:

PLAY THE CALDER GAME

TAKE FIVE

ALL ARE WELCOME

Calder Pillay peered inside, curious about what the Calder Game might be.

The walls and a series of floor-to-ceiling islands in the shape of irregular triangles, spheroids, and trapezoids were covered with red corkboard. In an alcove were round worktables surrounded by comfortable chairs, and in the middle of each table were stacks of thick drawing paper, a jar of mechanical pencils, and a basket of thumbtacks. The tables were blue, the chairs yellow. Calder, still not used to having to walk in a group, stepped into the room and read the directions, which were printed on a huge piece of posterboard:

Come in.

**We invite you to imagine and then record
a plan for a mobile made of anything you**

want to use: objects, symbols, or ideas. This mobile can exist only in thought, or it can be something that could be physically assembled. Design what you see, in your mind or in the world around you. As with any mobile, you are looking for balance, beauty, and surprise.

We ask only that your mobile have five parts that move in relation to one another. This is our way of putting together a unified and powerful show of your works, a show of your ideas, a show of fives!

Please share as many paper mobiles as you like. If you want to work on a design outside the museum and then return to post it on the walls, feel free to re-enter this room at any time.

All ages are invited.

Sponsored by the

FREE ART: SHARE IT!

Foundation

Wow, Calder thought to himself. Petra would love this — and so would Tommy, with his collector's eye. This was a way to make mobiles even if you didn't actually build them!

He'd just check it out, and then he'd catch up with the class. Maybe Ms. Button would let them all come back.

The Take Five room was filled with people drawing and posting and reading and smiling and discussing. In order to make it easier for people to play the game, the museum had printed up possible designs for those who might want them and left them in piles on the tables next to the blank paper. They had filled in examples, placing an X on the spot where each of the five mobile ingredients could go. The sample mobiles looked like this:

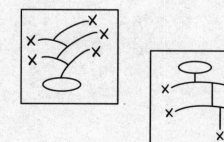

34

Calder ran his fingers over the designs, picturing pentominoes spinning in space. He noticed that people at the tables often started by using the MCA designs and then went on to organize their ideas in other ways.

"This is like eating popcorn, making these things," he heard one businessman exclaim as he sat at a table, his briefcase squashed under an elbow, busily adding to a pile of mobiles. "It's hard to stop!"

"It's like eating jellybeans," a nearby six-year-old added, then shrieked at an ear-splitting level, "Ma-mee! Come see what I *made*!"

"It's like someone turning you into an instant artist," a young man with tattoos said. "I love how you can say stuff, and then the people who look at it see other stuff."

Still busy with his pencil, the businessman grunted.

"I thought about it all day yesterday," an elderly woman cooed. "I had a marvelous idea in the middle of the night. I had to come back!"

Calder tried to see what she was making, but she covered it with her hand.

Then he noticed someone from the museum taking down a number of the paper mobiles from a crowded wall and laying them carefully in a box. "We'll do something wonderful with them later," she assured Calder. "We save every one!"

Suddenly realizing that a bit too much time had gone by, Calder hurried out. Perhaps this would be his heroic moment today: Ms. Button couldn't help but say yes to this room. Who could say no to such a great game?

⋀ ⋀ ⋀ "But you'll love it!" Calder sputtered.

Ms. Button, her mouth pulled flat like a zipper, said only, "We're already late for the gift shop. There's no way we're going to a game room, young man!"

Petra reached over and tweaked Calder's sleeve before he could say anything: Ms. Button was clearly hopeless. Calder, rarely angry, glowered and dug his hands deep into his pockets.

The seventh graders trooped into the gift

shop. A couple of kids bought postcards, but most stood in a depressed clump, waiting for the signal to leave. After so much real art, the cards looked flat. And a *gift shop* instead of a place where you could make your own mobile? What kind of a teacher *was* Ms. Button?

Calder, Tommy, and Petra looked in silence at a striking, black T-shirt with images of five red Alexander Calder sculptures. Arranged like letters across the front, the pieces could almost be symbols in a strange language. Calder Pillay was good at inventing codes, and the other two liked using them; ordinarily, the kids would have said something to one another, but not today.

The adult who had been watching earlier was now sitting on a bench inside the show, staring at a small mobile that had a handful of black wedge shapes and one red dot. Suddenly, as if swept away by a huge idea, this person clapped shut an overstuffed folder of papers, then jumped up and hurried in the direction of the Take Five room.

A lone receipt drifted to the floor. On the back were three words, written in a loopy scrawl:

Hunt for Creatures

Under that was one word:

Hang

The tail on the "g" slashed downward, as if pulled by a dreadful weight.

CHAPTER SIX

▲ ▲ ▲ When school was over that day, Calder, Petra, and Tommy headed for their old sixth-grade classroom. Enough was enough: They needed Ms. Hussey's help.

The three stood silently in the familiar door-way. All of them had baggy clothes and black hair, but Petra was several inches taller than Calder and a head taller than Tommy, making an odd staircase if they stood in the right order. Tommy's hair was shaggy and sat like a slippery shelf on the tops of his ears, Calder's was tough and bunchy, like the bristles on a worn scrub brush, and Petra's was long and puffy and forever trying to escape from a ponytail.

Ms. Hussey had her back to them, and was whistling cheerfully to herself. She was waist-deep in a tangle of wires, packing materials, and what looked like leftover family stuff: cups, shoes, cooking utensils, plastic animals, and boxes of board games.

On the wall facing the door were three

different posters of Alexander Calder's studio, showing what might have been the wildest work space of all time. Coils of wire, snippets and sheets of metal, tools, opened paint cans, and wooden crates covered every surface in a dense tumble of shapes and lines. It was impossible to tell where one object stopped and another began. In the middle was a head of scribbly, white hair bent over a shimmer of metal and a half-moon belly: Calder at work.

Ms. Hussey looked up, waved, and grinned. "Don't you love this photograph? Nothing can compare with the chaos in Calder's studio! And what a fabulous fall to be here in Chicago! The city is *glowing*! Didn't you adore the show today? What a thrill to see so many examples of what is probably the most original and profound art form of the twentieth century. I can hardly —" Ms. Hussey broke off, suddenly realizing how miserable the three kids looked.

"Hmm," she finished, putting down a giant pair of wire clippers. "Come in." She walked over and closed the classroom door behind them.

"So what's up?" she asked, although they knew that *she* knew. She crossed her arms. "It's hard for me, too, you know — I mean, to see my old sixth graders so unhappy. But that's the way school works, and there's not much any of us can do about it. There are highs and lows, and we're all supposed to keep moving."

"The Button wouldn't let us explore the show today, not on our own," Tommy muttered. "And I got in trouble for telling Calder I'd seen Goldman's tail."

"We weren't allowed to talk or write, and we couldn't stop for even a minute in the Take Five room," Petra said. "She made us go to the gift shop instead."

"And she confiscated my pentominoes," Calder reported in a flat tone. "She called them a toy."

A tiny, unhappy smile flickered across Ms. Hussey's eyes. She sank down on the top of a desk. "Sit," she ordered. They did.

She continued, "You can have a great year, I know it. You'll each just have to get used to being your own best starter. After all, that's kind of what grown-ups do." Ms. Hussey had twisted a piece of glittery party wire around her braid, and it bobbed in a saggy spiral on one side. She didn't look convinced. Suddenly, she shook her head.

"No, I can't say what I'm supposed to. Let's face it, Ms. Button is a — well, a challenge, but I know you three can handle it. Maybe you can even teach *her* a thing or two. And the good news is, you have one another." She looked at each of them, but no one nodded. "I'll try to give her a few hints. But right now, you have Alexander Calder to inspire you. How bad can things be?"

When there was still no answer but several swallowing sounds, Ms. Hussey hopped up. "Come on, I need some help here. We're collecting materials for mobile-building, but I've got to sort it out a bit or we'll be so crazy tomorrow that nobody will get anything done."

Tommy, Petra, and Calder each smiled at the thought, remembering happier times. Pretending not to notice, Ms. Hussey continued, "I thought

43

it was important to try actually doing what Alexander Calder did, balancing objects, before playing the Calder Game on paper."

Ms. Hussey dove back into the pile of what looked suspiciously like trash, and Calder, Petra, and Tommy followed her.

Soon the four were talking cheerfully about the Calder show.

"Amazing that he was an engineer, but one who invented his own, new structures to build," Calder mused. He had rescued a piece of garden trellis, and was now standing it on the toe of his sneaker.

"Exactly, he was highly trained in balancing weights but did something unexpected with what he'd learned," Petra said.

"And did you see those mobiles he first made, the ones with pieces of broken glass and wood and junk that he'd picked up? He was clearly a finder," Tommy said. He rummaged through a box of bathtub toys and old shoelaces.

"And a poet," Petra added, bending over an assortment of squashed party favors.

"I know you three are going to make many mobiles for the Calder Game exhibit, whether you do it in school or out." Ms. Hussey was sifting through a wooden crate filled with old gardening supplies. There were cracked tomato stakes, ancient packets of seeds, the wire fan of a rake — Ms. Hussey hunted thoughtfully, as if wanting to give each item a chance.

Tommy barked, "No time for making mobiles this fall, according to the Button."

"What?" Ms. Hussey said, momentarily confused. She frowned and stood up. "What did you say?"

"No time," Tommy repeated.

"Yeah, she said the Calder Game was a fun art project, but not for seventh graders who can't spell," Calder said.

"But if Ms. Button wants us to spell, why isn't she letting us write?" Petra blurted. "It doesn't make sense."

Ms. Hussey was quiet for a moment, then she straightened her shoulders. "Hey, I like that all of your mobiles will be so private," she said. "Who

45

knows what amazing stuff you'll come up with? I can't wait —" She paused, then shook her head. "I mean, I'd love to see them, any time."

"Great," Petra said, and felt like herself for the first time that day. Why was it that just being around Ms. Hussey was such a good thing? "We'll be back."

Ms. Hussey grinned, her familiar *we're-in-this-together-and-who-knows-where-it-will-take-us* look. "And, of course, you'll go back to the show on your own. Don't forget: You are never finished looking at a Calder mobile. Everything you see is shifting, in process — a sight that shouts, HERE! NOW! and reminds you that each second of your life holds its own world of experience."

Ms. Hussey paused for breath, and the three grinned. "So, there!" She nodded, hands on hips.

"Thanks," Calder said.

"Right," Tommy added, and squeezed a rubber duck he'd been holding. A squeaky *waaa* and drops of water came out.

"We won't forget," Petra promised.

▲ ▲ ▲ The following week, when Ms. Hussey heard about Calder's upcoming trip, she clapped her hands in delight. "How fabulous!" she beamed. "Since I can't go with you, I want you to do one thing for me."

She whispered something in Calder's ear, paused, then whispered some more. He nodded, his face serious.

When Petra and Tommy asked him what she'd said, he only shook his head and looked pleased. Neither could quite believe that Ms. Hussey had asked Calder to do something so secret. The moment felt funny, and not quite right.

What had Ms. Hussey said? And why couldn't Calder tell?

CHAPTER SEVEN

▲ ▲ ▲ Several days after Ms. Hussey whispered this secret in Calder's ear, on a Saturday afternoon in early October, the three kids stood outside Calder's house on Harper Avenue. Petra and Tommy were there to say good-bye; it was finally time for Calder and his dad to leave on their trip to England. The first autumn leaves dropped in slow, deliberate spirals, drifting with grace and abandon as if there were no tomorrows, no feet to squash and scuff them.

"Hey, mobiles everywhere," Petra said. "One moment they're happening, and the next they're not."

Neither boy replied. Calder squinted down the street, and his pentominoes — only returned yesterday by the Button — rattled busily as he stirred them in his pocket. Tommy kicked the curb and sighed.

"Ever collected leaves, Tommy?" Petra asked.

Tommy shook his head and stuck out his jaw. "Isn't that what we did in nursery school?" he asked. His voice implied that she should stop talking.

A little spurt of anger rose in Petra's throat, just enough to make her say meanly, "You also picked your nose in nursery school, and you still do *that*."

Both boys now looked at her. Petra turned her back on Tommy and said to Calder, "How about if you send me a mobile instead of a postcard? No words, and I'll try to figure it out."

"Okay," Calder said.

Tommy started to say something, opened his mouth, and shut it again.

A taxi pulled up, and the screen door behind them slammed. Calder's parents came out, and Yvette Pillay gave her son and then her husband many hugs. Her eyes were sad. Petra and Tommy glanced away.

"All right, boys!" she said. "Call when you arrive!"

Calder scrambled into the taxi first, and then his dad. As the car pulled away, Calder waved, a glint of yellow pentomino visible in his hand.

"I think that was a W," Petra said. "Or maybe an M for maze."

"It was an N," Tommy said gruffly.

Calder's mom sighed. "First time they've both been away," she said slowly, as if reminding herself of the facts. "At least they remembered their passports."

She looked at Petra and Tommy. "Stop by anytime, and I'll let you know the news," she said. Then, turning away with a worried smile, she walked back toward the house.

Petra glanced at Tommy, wondering if they would even say two words to each other without Calder around. Tommy's shoulders were hunched, as if he'd shrunk.

"See you," he said, then stared straight ahead, which happened to be right at Petra's neck. "Going this way?" he asked. Without waiting for an answer, he spun around and began to walk.

Petra stared for a moment at his back, then hurried off in the opposite direction.

"Little *jerk*," she muttered angrily to herself.

"Stupid *girl*, thinks she has all the ideas," Tommy said under his breath.

Both ached, suddenly, for Calder's company, and at the same time felt relieved that things were out in the open: They weren't going to pretend to get along while Calder was gone.

Yvette Pillay, peering out at the empty street moments later, sighed. Maybe she'd go back to the wonderful Alexander Calder exhibit today. Mobiles were healing. They always seemed to sing, *Look, no tangles, we do what we want, yet here we all are*. A mobile is simply an ideal family, she thought, reaching for her jacket. Everyone moves and changes, but in reality they all stay connected.

Look, no tangles, we do what we want. The words had a catchy rhythm.

Walking along Harper Avenue to the train station, she glanced back at their house, which was the only red building on the block. Had she locked the door? Of course! Admiring the

airborne yellows caught between the bright
rectangle of their home and the dark slashes of
trees, she tried hard to ignore a sense of something hovering — something frightening that did
not fit.

CHAPTER EIGHT

▲ ▲ ▲ When he arrived in London the next morning, Calder was in a daze. He was so excited that he'd stayed awake for almost the entire flight. This was a first, leaving the United States, and he didn't want to miss a thing.

As the plane landed, he checked the sky and clouds to see if they looked different. He thought they did; they were mixed together into a smooth gray that made him think of a gummy eraser, the kind Ms. Hussey used in projects. And the accents! Even in the airport, Calder felt an immediate and confusing shock of recognition. His grandma Ranjana, who had died three years before, had spoken English with a British accent, and his dad had just the slightest trace of the same sound in his voice. Amazing how a person's language can change the way you see them, Calder thought to himself.

As his dad hunted for the luggage, Calder sank down in the baggage area and continued to stare. What *was* a foreigner, anyway? Is the place you're born the only place you really belong? That seemed ridiculous. He knew lots of people who had been born other places but were definitely not foreigners in the United States — after all, his mom was from Canada and his dad was from India. Calder had been born in Hyde Park, but he couldn't see that it made any difference.

Most of the people he liked had family in other parts of the world. Tommy had been born in Colombia, his father's country, and his mom was from England, although she hadn't been back for a long time. Petra had family in the Middle East, in North Africa, and in Europe. Calder had no idea where she'd been born, and it had never occurred to him to ask.

He wondered: At what point do you stop being from "away" and start being from "here"? Ms. Hussey would like puzzling over this whole idea.

His dad seemed happy to be surrounded by British voices. He'd found their bags, and now walked quickly and smiled lots. Soon they climbed on the bus to Oxford and Calder sat by the window, watching the scenery turn quickly to rolling hills and small roads. Yellow and red leaves, tiny discs and crescents, dotted the green. Hey, parts of a huge Calder mobile, he thought to himself, and wished Petra was there to share the idea. She loved it when art turned up in the real world. He noticed that the clock on the bus was on twenty-four-hour time: It read 16:44.

He elbowed his dad. "Are clocks always like that over here?" he asked.

"Yes, when transportation is involved. Very logical, don't you think?"

Calder nodded. A moment later he saw a sign that said SOFT VERGES, followed by QUEUE CAUTION. He elbowed his dad, who explained that the first meant *swampy ground by the edge of the road*, and the second meant *traffic ahead*. Both British signs seemed so gentle and polite. Then Calder thought again of his grandma, who sometimes used that word *queue* in the grocery store in Chicago, when she really meant *line*. How could a line be a Q, if one was straight and the other curly? It had always made Calder giggle, the idea of people waiting in a Q with their eggs and milk.

Before long Calder and his dad arrived in Oxford and changed buses for Woodstock, the town where they were staying. On the second bus, Calder's eyes began to droop, and he slept.

▲ ▲ ▲ A short time later, Calder's dad patted his shoulder. "We're here," he said.

The bus left them on a street corner in front of a row of stone houses. Walter Pillay pulled out a map, handed it to Calder, and said, "We're looking for the Knowsley Bed-and-Breakfast, on Alehouse Lane."

They studied the map together, then bump-bumped their suitcases across the street, around a corner, and down a short, curved alley. Everything seemed very quiet and very old. It was beginning to get dark, and a soft drizzle was falling. Calder noticed there weren't many street-lights. He and his father turned another corner, and stopped dead.

57

They had found the town square, but something was wrong. Both father and son froze, and neither said a word for several seconds.

Calder's dad had picked what he'd hoped was a typical English town for them to stay in, a sleepy place that belonged to another century and another, slower time. But what was this?

In the middle of the empty square was a gigantic, red sculpture. It was extraordinary, exuberant, and unmistakable — could this possibly be a piece of art by Alexander Calder? What was it doing here?

"Bizarre," Calder's dad said, and Calder understood the note of confusion in his voice. After all, had they come all this way to see something they could have seen at home?

As soon as they knocked on Miss Posy Knowsley's door, it flew open. Had she been waiting on the other side? Her speed was a little mysterious. An older woman with a pillowy figure, she spun away and whisked them upstairs to their room before they'd had a chance even to shake hands. She then shut the bedroom door with what was almost a bang.

Their room smelled like roses and had several embroidered pillows that said things like *Walk softly and carry a big bag* and *The early bird gets the bird*. There was a small lamp in the shape of an overflowing treasure chest, complete with skull and crossbones, between the beds. Calder and his dad kicked off their shoes and flopped down on top of the covers, too tired to wonder at the weird sayings or even to wash.

As Calder drifted off that night, his dad already asleep nearby, he thought of what Ms. Hussey had whispered to him. Then he listened to the *splat-splat* of water dripping steadily on stone, and pictured Alexander Calder's red metal gleaming oddly under a damp English moon.

⋀ ⋀ ⋀ The next morning they tiptoed downstairs and found a table set for two in the front parlor. Miss Knowsley popped out of the kitchen in her slippers, and this time they had a chance to look at her. She had blue glasses, a tricky apron covered with small suitcases stacked in a checkerboard pattern, and hair that reminded Calder of dough. Although Calder knew her last name began with a K, he wondered if there was anything remarkable about her nose. There wasn't.

She served them fried eggs with both bacon and sausage, as well as a plate of very dry toast. Calder wasn't used to all the fat in the meat, and pushed it carefully to one side. While his dad ate, Calder looked around the room.

There were ten sets of china salt and pepper shakers on shelves, exactly twenty pottery beer mugs, three candy dishes sitting on lace on round side tables, a basket filled with many pairs of knitting needles and red balls of wool, lots and lots of old group photographs, and five fancy paintings, also of people.

Calder was staring, looking from one portrait to the next. Several of the men had something resembling a wool pancake on their heads. Calder wanted to point this out to his dad, but Miss

Knowsley was watching them from the doorway, sliding her hands around and around each other as if washing them in air.

"Oh, yes, family in their Sunday best," Miss Knowsley said, as if it were obvious. "Generations and generations. I was born in this house. It's been a struggle to stay here, what with taxes and repairs, but I've never lived anyplace else. Nor will I."

Calder's dad looked up quickly, perhaps afraid Calder might say "Weird," something that often popped out while his son was thinking. Sausage in one cheek, Walter Pillay said, "Tell us about the Calder sculpture. It is a Calder, isn't it?"

Miss Knowsley's pleased expression vanished. As Calder watched, fascinated, her face went from sweet to severe. "We aren't happy about it here in Woodstock," she said with a scowl. "It's been in the square for a couple of weeks now, and created quite the uproar. Given to the town anonymously this fall, some say by a rich American. He apparently has other pieces of modern art. A *gift*, he called it, but I think he must have been cleaning out his tractor barn. Valuable, I'm sure. I guess that impresses some people."

She paused, perhaps remembering that her guests were also American. "At any rate," she said brusquely, turning away. A *scrape-slam-slam* sound came from the kitchen.

"Oh, that'll be Pummy," Miss Knowsley said, brightening. "He comes and goes on his own. Smartest cat in town."

She opened the swing door to the kitchen. "Come, Pummy dear! Come to Mummy! Come at once. We have visitors."

Calder and his dad watched as an immense, black barrel of fur rolled toward them. One beady, amber eye blinked up from the end of the barrel; the other eye was closed in a permanent wink. It was hard to believe that Pummy could stand.

"*Yeow*," the shape said.

"Yes, poor dear, lost an eye in an accident as a baby," Miss Knowsley said tenderly, bending over to pat the cat on the side like a small dog. "That's my boy, Pummy! He comes and goes through his own door in the back, but when I see him in town and say, 'Home, Pummy, Home!' he turns right around and trots back. Amazing, really. *Such* an intelligent boy."

"*Yeow*," Pummy said again. He was sitting now, and waves of furry belly rolled outward around his front paws. He looked impatiently in the direction of the breakfast dishes, and then at Miss Knowsley. No wonder he hurries home, Calder thought to himself.

As Miss Knowsley cleared the table, Pummy rolled along in her wake, yeowling piteously. "Yes, dear," the older woman said, holding open the kitchen door with her elbow so Pummy could enter first.

As Calder and his dad left the house ten minutes later, Miss Knowsley handed the boy a key on a metal ring. Its worn lettering read, *Visit Woodstock, Home of Kings*. Calder popped it into his pocket and heard it make an unfamiliar clink against his set of pentominoes.

"What's in that pocket, anyway?" Miss Knowsley asked, her face close to Calder's. Her glasses were very thick. "An entire toolbox?"

"Pentominoes," Calder said stiffly, pulling out the V piece to show her.

"I see," she said, but clearly didn't. "Now, young man: I know your dad will be off during the day, and you may want to come and go." Opening her eyes very wide, she gave Calder a calculating look. Her eyes slid back and forth behind him, as if something in the corners needed watching.

"Guard my key," Miss Knowsley continued. "Who knows *who* may be coming through town, what with that monstrosity out there."

It was shocking for Calder to hear an Alexander Calder sculpture referred to as monstrous. He and his father smiled weakly and nodded. Calder decided she must have forgotten what his name was. Either that, or she didn't want to remember.

As he followed his dad out the door, Calder stepped carefully over Pummy. The cat was lying down now and filled most of the hall. He stopped licking his front paw and looked furiously at Calder, the tip of his tongue sticking out, as if to say, "Not a word about all that bacon, understand?"

Calder smiled and reached out to give Pummy a scratch behind the ear. *Whang!* Before the boy could touch him, Pummy gave Calder a surprisingly hard whack on the hand, a warning with just a hint of claws.

Calder quickly shut the door.

CHAPTER NINE

▲ ▲ ▲ While his dad attended the first day of the conference at the Oxford Botanic Garden, Calder wandered around. The place was a marvel. Started almost four hundred years before, it was the oldest medicinal garden in Europe, and Calder knew that it was filled with rare plants that had been brought back to England from all over the world. Calder was used to his dad, whose job was to make gardens in cities, trying out plants in their front yard, but this was something else. Stretching in all directions were long rectangles filled with leaves and flowers, row after row, the beds set in a smooth carpet of green grass. Outside the garden's high stone walls, traffic flew by; inside, all was leafy and peaceful.

Calder noticed that the plants were divided into families. He passed the ivies, then found himself admiring a clump of delicate, red lanterns, labeled *Physalis alkekengi*. Suddenly, he was in front of a dark, scrubby plant called *Ruscaceae,* or butcher's broom. A broom to sweep away meat, or maybe blood? Calder's eyebrows went up, and he looked further — this was getting interesting. Next was *Papaver somniferum*, or the opium poppy. Small letters said, SOURCE OF MORPHINE AND CODEINE. Wow — Calder glanced around. This was toxic stuff, and no one was looking to see if you picked any.

He wandered on, feeling guilty for having a thought like that. Maybe people in England were just more trustworthy. And look at this! Calder knelt down, wanting to be sure he was reading correctly: belladonna! Wasn't that a deadly poison? The leaves were a gentle, lettucey green, and Calder found himself thinking it would be easy, if you wanted to murder someone, to mix a few in with a salad. Wouldn't Tommy be thrilled if he brought a leaf back! But suddenly Calder pictured a scene at the airport in which he and his dad were arrested and thrown in prison on smuggling charges or worse, and his mom was saying through the bars, *What on Earth were you thinking?*

Next he passed a sign for stonecrops and houseleeks, then bleeding hearts, which he knew from the gardens at home. Now came pinks and soapworts. And a greenhouse filled with cacti of all kinds, some so tiny that there were magnifying glasses left around for interested lookers.

Again, in the greenhouses, Calder saw no guards or officials of any kind. What an honest place. He was beginning to really like England. And what was this? A small green sign said, PLANT PROBLEMS SOLVED: MAN EATER. Calder resisted the temptation to try a finger in front of one of the blossoms. Instead, he stirred his pentominoes happily as he walked on. This place was awesome.

Outside the greenhouses, he wandered to the edge of a small river that had flat-bottomed, rectangular boats pushed off to one side. Calder had noticed that the English streets and sidewalks were rarely in straight lines, unlike the ones in Chicago, and yet here was a boat in the shape of a regular polygon, a boat with hardly a curve anywhere. The English certainly had some unusual ideas.

The river looked like something from a picture that Petra had glued to the back of her notebook, and suddenly Calder wished with all his heart that his two friends could be there with him. Petra would be writing on a bench, Tommy would no doubt be looking for treasure, and the three would be talking about things like Miss Knowsley's cat and the strangely dangerous garden. Calder sighed.

His dad had given him a map of Oxford and had showed him where to go for lunch and how to get to Christ Church, where Lewis Carroll had worked and lived. Calder had never been a big fan of *Alice's Adventures in Wonderland*, even though he knew Lewis Carroll was a terrific mathematician and had loved playing with numbers. Maybe it was just that Alice was always bursting into tears. When his parents had read the book aloud to him, Calder had fidgeted and wondered about all the crying. Maybe Alice would have stayed calmer if she'd had a set of pentominoes in her pocket; she'd clearly needed something to focus on.

The Oxford campus looked a little like an older version of the University of Chicago, which was right in his neighborhood in Hyde Park. His dad had told him that the name Hyde Park was really borrowed from a park in London, and now he could see that lots of the campus architecture at home had been borrowed, too. There were carvings and gargoyles along the tops of buildings and around doorways, but the stone in Oxford was a brighter color, something between popcorn and mustard. Corners of the English buildings were worn round in places, and the stone was chipped and scarred.

Calder's dad had said that Oxford was the oldest university in the English-speaking world. It had been started close to a thousand years earlier. He ran his hand along an especially beat-up wall and thought about how new everything was in the United States. He was standing on a street that people had walked over for century after century. What had this wall seen? Had anyone been killed on this street? Or right on this spot? It made his scalp tingle, thinking about all the people, good and bad, who had come and gone over so many years, and all the ideas that had gotten them excited or mad or worried.

Bells seemed to ring every ten minutes. He got lost three times on the way to Christ Church, and then found the building was closed for renovation. Back on the sidewalk outside the botanic garden, a chaotic combination of students, faculty, and tourists streamed in all directions. Calder realized he was starving, and ducked into a sandwich shop. There was a long line, and when he got to the front and tried to order a hamburger and fries with ketchup, the person behind the counter said, "Sorry? Was that a beef burger in a bap with chips?"

Calder had no idea, and he felt his neck getting hot with embarrassment. What on earth was a "bap"? And what about the fries? He stirred the pentominoes in his pocket so vigorously that one fell underfoot. Diving down to retrieve it, he cracked his head on the counter. As people huffed impatiently behind him, he pointed miserably to a cucumber sandwich and some lemonade.

He hoped this would be the last awkward moment of the trip, but a dark, jumpy feeling inside told him it wasn't going to be.

"Keep wishing," he whispered to himself, then frowned. The words had an oddly nasty sound.

CHAPTER TEN

▲ ▲ ▲ Even after lunch, the main streets were choked with buses and trucks and cars and bicycles. It was hectic in comparison to Woodstock and to his neighborhood at home. Calder went back into the botanic garden to wait for his dad.

He lay down under a tree and pulled out his pentominoes. Just the sight of them was soothing. Resting his head on his arm, he closed his eyes for a moment. Chicago was six hours earlier and four time zones away; if he were home, he wouldn't even be awake yet. Soon his mind filled with colorful dreams about cutting belladonna leaves into the shape of pentominoes and making a twelve-piece rectangle that Pummy wanted to eat.

"NO, Pummy! Poison!" he remembered saying. By the time he'd lured Pummy to another part of the garden with a snack, careful to stay out of range, his belladonna masterpiece had blown away. Then, in the dream, Calder decided to count and sort all the rectangles he could remember, beginning with the gardens and the odd boats and going on to the cucumber sandwiches, and —

"Calder? How was your day?" His father was crouching next to him in the garden. As they walked back to the bus station that afternoon, he told his dad about the dream.

"Sounds like an *Alice* event," Walter Pillay said with a smile. "Maybe it's Lewis Carroll's ghost getting into your brain. Not that you're anything like Alice."

"I hope not," Calder said.

"What did you do to your head?"

"A little accident at lunchtime," Calder said.

"Ah." His dad looked at him, waiting for more. Calder was quiet. "But you managed," his dad offered.

Calder nodded, realizing suddenly that this might be the first day he had spent by himself and in an unfamiliar place. Ever. Of course he'd felt a bit strange! He stood up straighter.

▲ ▲ ▲ The quiet stone houses in Woodstock were a relief. As Calder and his dad headed back to the bed-and-breakfast, an old man in suspenders and slippers shuffled across the street with an even older dog. Neither looked for cars. Wind rattled a loose window. Dry leaves rustled underfoot. Calder thought of one of his elderly neighbors in Hyde Park.

"Mrs. Sharpe would love it here," he remarked. As far as he could tell, Louise Coffin Sharpe liked everything old — houses, furniture, and books. Even ideas.

"*Mmm*, she'd fit right in," his dad agreed.

"Think I'll stay here tomorrow, Dad."

Walter Pillay looked at his son. "Good plan. It's a bit like Hyde Park, isn't it? But a much more mysterious Hyde Park — one that has seen kings and queens and countless dramas. We'll bring the map and that Woodstock guide book with us to dinner and see what we can find out."

"It's partly the high walls that make it so mysterious," Calder added.

As if to illustrate his point, they heard the

sudden *scritch-clink* sounds of someone digging in pebbly dirt with a metal tool, someone on the other side of a wall that rose above their heads.

"A late gardener getting his bulbs in," Calder's dad suggested.

"Or maybe someone digging up treasure," Calder said, thinking of Tommy.

As they approached Alehouse Lane, both peered around a parked truck toward the sculpture, which still felt shocking; it looked so wild and bright in a setting that seemed to celebrate the worn and the private.

At that moment, a young girl dressed in black pants and a sweatshirt also peered out, from the far side of the town square. After a quick look in all directions, she flew toward the sculpture. She had long, pipe-thin legs like a shorebird, a dusting of sandy hair, and a delicate nose like a beak. Calder and his dad froze, somehow knowing that they'd intrude if they stepped into view. Circling the Calder sculpture at top speed, the girl held up a small camera and snapped at least ten pictures. She then popped

the camera back in her pocket and pulled out a measuring tape.

A pub door down the street opened with a heavy thump, and a roar of rumbly laughter drifted out. Calder and his dad heard someone shout, "I'm not DAFT! Ripstapore mumfi-dumble RIP!"

The door swung shut, cutting off the rest of the bellow.

The girl froze for a moment, one arm extended, then whipped the tape hurriedly into a pocket and sat down on a bench. She pulled out a pen and paper and began to draw on one knee, her head bent over her lap.

Calder and Walter Pillay heard heavy foot-steps and stepped out from behind the truck. A giant man was striding from the pub toward the girl.

"What did I tell you?" he growled. It was the same voice. "You're not to be near here! Not now, not EVER!"

The girl shrugged and kept drawing, as if she'd been sitting there for ages.

Suddenly, the man lunged forward, grabbed the piece of paper, scrunched it in one massive fist, and tossed it under the bench.

The girl froze for a second time, holding the pencil as if she were still using it.

"No daughter of mine will turn a deaf ear!" he shouted.

Without a word, the girl stood. She turned and walked stiffly away from the square, disappearing down a narrow lane.

The man, still breathing heavily, looked at the darkening blue overhead and hunched his shoulders as if it were cold. Then he shrugged and strode after the girl, a low burble of angry words drifting behind him like the wake behind a boat. He vanished down the same lane.

"Not the nicest of dads," Calder said.

"No, but he was worried," Walter Pillay mused. "I wonder why?"

"This atmosphere of secrets kind of pulls you in," Calder added.

Walter Pillay nodded. "Harmless, though. That is, until someone gets murdered . . ."

"Dad!"

"Just kidding."

While Calder struggled to open Miss Knowsley's door with her giant key, his father looked up at the rooftops and sky and sighed. "Amazing spot," he murmured.

As father and son stepped inside, a face shaped like an ax peered out from behind a curtain across the street. Dark eyes blinked, and the fabric fell back in place.

CHAPTER ELEVEN

⋀ ⋀ ⋀ After saying good-bye to his dad at the bus the next morning, Calder shoved both hands deep in his pockets and set off across town.

He'd decided on the Start Small, Move to Large approach that his Grandma Ranjana had taught him. It seemed to work with almost everything in life. After all, you couldn't leap to making twelve-piece pentomino rectangles when you'd never made a five-piece one.

"Very mature of you," his father had agreed, when Calder told him that he wanted to get to know the town today and save the maze and Blenheim for tomorrow.

Although it only dated back to 1991, the maze pictured history: It symbolized the Duke of Marlborough's famous eighteenth-century victory in Blenheim, Bavaria, an important battle won for the Queen of England. Some said the maze was the largest puzzle of its kind in the world. Calder knew the design included trumpets, banners, cannonballs, and even a cannon. He wasn't sure how you get lost in a bunch of symbols made from bushes, but he'd find out. He stirred his pentominoes eagerly at the thought of it.

When he passed a diagram of the maze in a shop window, he was careful to look away. He didn't want any clues. Besides, he had some good pentomino maze ideas going, puzzles he'd been working on during the flight, and he wanted to get them straight before walking into the Marlborough maze. Better not to get the two confused.

Although Calder had planned to explore on his own, actually doing it felt a little weird. Compared to Oxford, there weren't many people, and everyone here was amazingly pale, as if they hadn't been in the sun in years. Most glanced at Calder and then looked away. Were they hiding something? Or did he look funny? Calder surreptitiously checked the zipper on his pants.

He wandered down one twisty street after another. Hadn't he just been down this lane? But no, here were stores he'd never passed before, each window jammed with interesting stuff. One held the dangly parts of old chandeliers and a row of glass doorknobs; another candlesticks with curly handles; now pajama-striped gardening gloves, eggcups made from the heads of kings, and a shelf of teapots plastered with intricate flower patterns. A blackboard propped against a building advertised a "brace of dressed pheasant" and "dressed" wild duck, partridge, guinea fowl, quail, and pigeon. There was also "oven ready" wild rabbit and wild hare. Did *dressed* really mean *naked* here? And what was a *brace?* He peeked in the butcher's window at a row of birds hanging by their necks, and also identified a small pink foot with no fur. He shuddered, glad that meat at home was rarely recognizable.

Hey! What was this? He'd found some old wooden stocks. Stocks for humiliating people who broke the law. How nasty! There was a narrow bench to sit on, and a place where your ankles got clamped between two heavy pieces of wood. There you sat, imprisoned for all to see. It must have felt terrible. He counted five ankle-holes. Was that for two thieves with two legs and one with only one? If Tommy were going to school here, the Button would probably have him in the stocks all the time.

Passing the stocks, Calder walked into the Oxfordshire Museum. Miss Knowsley had insisted that it was "Just the place to start, so much for a boy to see!" The building was yet another old stone house. He'd be able to walk through quickly if it was all glass cases filled with dishes and jewelry.

But it wasn't. The first room he stopped in was filled with stuffed animals and skeletons. These creatures had all lived here at one time — suddenly Calder pictured them running through the streets. He looked at the woolly mammoth jaws, and at the tusks and bones and teeth of ancient elephants, bison, bears, and even a lion. Apparently some 200,000 years ago, the climate had been warmer. Then there were the more recent wild mammals: a fox, a hare, a hedgehog, a weasel, stoats, voles, moles, a stag, squirrels, field mice and rats, even some unidentified human skulls. And the birds: Calder read crazy names

TAKE NOTICE
MEN TRAPS and SPRING
GUNS ARE SET ON THESE
PREMISES

like pied wagtail, jack snipe, greenshank, and great crested grebe. Hundreds of glassy eyes peered out at him. A sign told him that this part of England was known as the Cotswolds and had been densely wooded for many centuries. Clearly, it was still home to countless creatures. Calder pictured a stuffed Pummy, fur bristling, his one eye gleaming. He'd fit right in.

Poachers and Gamekeepers was the next exhibit. Calder knew that poachers stole and gamekeepers were hired to protect. A few years ago, he'd read Roald Dahl's book, *Danny the Champion of the World*. Set in a small English village, it made clear that poaching pheasants was a time-honored art and also a rather scary game. Now this was interesting: Here were some very old guns, a giant bow and arrow, and a bunch of wicked traps that were meant to catch the poachers. One, labeled MAN TRAP, was made of iron and used from around 1750 to 1827, when it was outlawed as being too cruel. It could break a man's leg, arm, or worse — and it was usually hidden in bushes. Calder read more, this from 1809:

"The vicinity is filled with poachers, deer stealers, thieves, and pilferers of every kind; offenses of almost every description abound so much that the offenders are a terror to all quiet and well-disposed persons. Oxford gaol would be uninhabited were it not for this fertile source of crime."

Somehow, Calder remembered that *gaol* was the English word for *jail*. Hmm, so at one time there were lots of desperate and daring people hiding in this neighborhood, and lots of animals to hunt if you were needy enough to risk your life, or at least one of your hands or feet. The punishments were probably vicious if you got caught unharmed. Calder imagined there were even nastier ones than the ones mentioned in the exhibit. Clearly, the poachers and the wealthy landowners were two different kinds of people, and neither felt much pity for the other. This was a darker side to English life than he had seen yesterday in the botanic garden.

Calder thought suddenly of the unseen shovel digging away on the other side of an ancient wall, of the Angry Dad, and of his gruff voice. It had sounded like a voice that could make or break its own rules. Would Angry Dad have been a poacher or a gamekeeper?

This was one game Calder did not want to play.

CHAPTER TWELVE

▲ ▲ ▲ Once outside the museum, Calder decided he'd had enough of the past, at least for the moment. He spotted a small card shop that was also a post office. He'd buy three stamps and send postcards to his mom, Petra, and Tommy. He crossed the street, stepping on each of several huge, yellow leaves that had blown here and there across the cobbles — Petra would say they looked like stars, and Tommy would then roll his eyes. Smiling at the thought, Calder ducked inside the door of the shop and looked around.

A group of adults stood in a cluster by the newspapers and cards. Calder saw a counter with a small window labeled ROYAL MAIL in the corner. A man sat on a stool behind the window, waiting for customers. It was by far the smallest post office Calder had ever seen.

He was busy for several minutes picking out cards, and then realized that the shop was quiet — too quiet. He glanced up, and then down again. *Squeak-squeak* went the rack, and

Calder plunged one hand into his pentominoes pocket.

A middle-aged woman peered suspiciously around the cards, perhaps seeing the boy's hand slide into his pocket. One of the older men cleared his throat, as if he'd been interrupted and was ready to continue.

He poked a finger into one ear, jiggled it vigorously, then barked, "Monstrous!"

The woman gave a loud, impatient sigh that made Calder think of a hen's *bawk*. "Yes, oh dear, *bawk,* most unpleasant. Perhaps if it had been a smaller variety." She then paused to shuffle through a stack of papers, as if the topic wasn't important enough to discuss any longer.

A third voice chimed in. The speaker's words sounded mushy, as though his mouth was numb — Calder wondered if he'd just come from the dentist. "Well, that's the pity of it, no one asked us, did they? No consideration, but then *those* people don't know any better. What's good for them is also good for everyone else. Never mind if the shoe doesn't fit!"

The woman's voice now scolded, "Peckish, that's what you all are! Haven't you watched any of those museum shows on the telly? It's a donation, didn't cost us a penny! And it's ever so colorful!"

The ear-cleaner now grunted. "Right, about as artful as what's stuck to my finger," he muttered. There was a wave of *tut*s, *tsk*s, a *bawk*, and several nose-snorts.

Smiling, Calder joined in with what he thought was a soft *hah* — and instantly there was total silence. Wishing he'd stayed quiet, he rushed his three cards into a corner and got busy.

He'd just printed *Dear Mom,* when a new voice boomed into the shop.

"Well?" the man shouted. "With or against?" No one replied, and the man went on, "Cat got your tongues? Well, you can all rot down under before I'll allow it! That's been our square for countless generations! I'll do the job myself if I have to!"

"Nashy," the Ear Man warned. "Hang it up."

Calder was now hardly breathing, and stared

miserably at the counter beneath his hand. It was the Angry Dad from the square! And his name was Nashy — just like gnashing teeth. What was the fastest way out? Now that he'd written on one of the cards, he couldn't put it back. He stepped over to the ROYAL MAIL window.

The newcomer bellowed, "I'll hang *you* up — dressed and all!"

Calder thought for a dreadful split second that the man was talking to him, but then realized that the target was Ear Man.

"Three postcard stamps, please," Calder murmured, thinking suddenly of the dead and very naked birds hanging in the butcher's window.

The person selling asked, "For?"

Calder paused, thinking he'd give anything to disappear. "The United States," he whispered. The silence was now dreadful.

Calder's hands were sweating and his heart pounding by the time he reached for his money and stuffed everything roughly into his back pocket. As he turned to go, he realized the man who'd been shouting was now blocking the door.

Nashy was built like a bull and had a heavy ridge of bone on his brow. Wiry, ginger-colored hair sprouted from every side of his neck, and dense bristles poked from both nostrils, making two tiny brooms. He was the hairiest man Calder had ever seen. The name Nashy seemed too human; Angry Dad fit him better.

He gave the giant man a half-smile, as if to say, *I'm American but not that kind*, and the man gave him a long, mean stare. Did he recognize Calder from the day before?

He moved just enough for Calder to slip by, and then banged the side of the door with his fist as the boy walked away. Calder jumped.

"Now, Nashy . . ." It was Slush Mouth speaking this time.

The man growled something unpleasant in response, something that ended "*oh-ta-da-bahg.*"

Calder's stomach churned as he crossed the square. He noticed that the piece of paper that had been tossed under the bench yesterday was now gone. Passing the sculpture, he reached out and gave it a quick pat, as if telling it not to worry.

Then he glanced back at the post office, which now looked empty.

A lone, yellow leaf drifted down in front of the open door, landing gently in the cradle of the sill. A woman hopped off a blue bicycle and stepped carefully around the leaf, adjusting the soft rectangle of the plastic bag on her shoulder. Calder had noticed that everyone in Woodstock carried those saggy bags.

Bag! Suddenly, the boy realized what Angry Dad had said.

Out of the bag . . . poachers carried bags. What or who had gotten out of Angry Dad's bag? *Don't let the cat out of the bag.* Calder knew the expression meant *don't give away the secret.* He imagined Pummy in a bag and shuddered.

The secret had something to do with the huge sculpture, Calder was sure of that. But why was everybody so upset about a piece of art, one they hadn't even paid for? He understood them not liking it, but why the fury?

Calder was beginning to realize that outsiders who interfered weren't too popular, and that

Woodstock residents were used to defending their own territory. He guessed that people, like the streets and houses, hadn't changed much in Woodstock over the past several hundred years. No wild animals running by, but the same basic ideas. And what about the same games?

He thought again about the Man Trap, and wondered if several centuries ago there had been a number of residents missing a foot or even an arm. Had they behaved like Angry Dad?

Calder wandered past two fieldstone churches, both with graveyards, and then found himself standing in front of another. He opened the wrought-iron gate and stepped inside. Perfect: A little time with his mazes, away from shops and streets. He'd finish the cards later. He certainly wasn't going back into the post office today.

The graveyard was long and thin, an odd shape, and houses had been built right to the edges on three sides. Calder spotted a window with a jar of toothbrushes and a tidy row of bottles and tubes along the sill. What was it like to brush your teeth in the morning and look out at a backyard filled with bodies? He scanned the windows: Good, no one in sight.

Gravestones packed the space but not in rows, and in places there was only a foot or two between the markers. How did *that* work? Streaky and spotted with lichen, the stones leaned in every direction. Even the tombs were lopsided, some sinking into the ground. Calder had never seen such a crazy-looking graveyard; it made him think of a bunch of birthday candles stuck in a cake by a very young child.

Well, at least it was private in here, and almost cheerful in the middle of the day. Calder walked over to a low tomb. The lettering on it was so worn that it had almost disappeared. Pulling his hand into the sleeve of his sweatshirt, he whisked a place clean of berries and twigs, and then unloaded the pentominoes in his pocket. He also pulled out a wad of graph paper and three mechanical pencils, the cheapest kind from the grocery store at home. Those were the best.

Soon he was sitting happily on the slab of stone, one leg tucked beneath him. He hummed quietly to himself as he moved his pentominoes around, occasionally flipping one over.

Every once in a while he'd release an *ah-ha* kind of sound and begin to draw, glancing at the pentomino arrangement as he worked. The first thing he made looked like this:

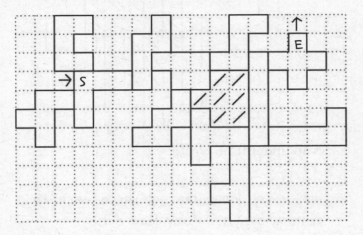

Under it, he wrote:

I'm pritending these mazes are surrounded by a rectangle of solid hedge, and that what you're looking at is the path. This one has 7 dead-ends and 1 loop. A dead-end has to have 2 turns in it.

The next looked like this:

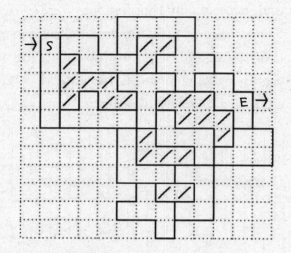

And under it he wrote:

How many loops can you have using 12 pentominoes? How many dead-ends?

Almost an hour had gone by since he sat down, and after recording the second maze, he stretched his arms over his head and looked around.

A huge black crow hopped slowly along the top of the brick wall that separated the graveyard from the houses. Every once in a while it stopped to peck at the moss on the wall. It now turned to face Calder, spread its wings, and flew directly toward him.

Calder ducked, and the crow flapped heavily overhead. He was glad he wasn't superstitious — well, *too* superstitious. Everyone was a tiny bit, if they admitted it.

Didn't crows have something to do with death?

CHAPTER THIRTEEN

▲ ▲ ▲ There was no one walking on the sidewalk, and no sign of life in the houses. There might be more dead people in this town than living, Calder thought to himself. Leaving the graveyard, he stepped on each of the rectangular flagstones in the sidewalk, hopping lightly over the irregular shapes.

The night before, he and his dad had spotted a place called the Lyon Tea Shop that had a menu in the window. There were no burgers or hot dogs, but there were tuna fish sandwiches, which Calder loved. His dad had suggested that he go there for lunch.

Calder opened the door and stumbled inside; the room was dark, and the floor was not exactly even. He had an impression of small, round tables with people seated at most of them, a buzz of conversation, and a counter at the front.

"What'll it be?" The girl behind the counter snapped a drawer shut, and Calder looked up. He was shocked to see Bird Girl — the one who had been taking pictures of the Calder sculpture. Still wearing black, she was all elbows and wrists; even her chin looked sharp. She might be a year or two older than Calder, but wasn't any taller. Studying Calder with a steady, gray gaze, she didn't show any sign of interest or recognition.

Relieved, Calder ordered a tuna with chips, having learned that they were what Americans called fries, and a large chocolate milk with extra syrup.

"Name?" the girl asked.

"Calder," he said.

At that, he saw her blink several times, then glance quickly behind him. The restaurant suddenly felt quiet. The girl spun around and disappeared through a swing door to the kitchen.

Calder plopped down at one of the tables. Was he imagining it, or was everyone in the restaurant looking at him?

He slunk down in his seat, pulled out his wad of graph paper, and peered over the top of it. Yikes — there was Ear Man at a nearby table! And Hen Voice and Slush Mouth, also from the post office. They leaned toward each other and whispered something, then both glanced in his direction.

Calder turned his chair away, only to find that he was then facing a giant set of shoulders and a great, hairy arm. Could there be two men that size in Woodstock? Maybe, but not two men with that amount of hair on every imaginable surface. Luckily, Angry Dad was reading his mail and didn't seem to have noticed Calder — yet.

On the other side of him, a man wearing blue jeans, a black leather jacket, and sunglasses snapped open a copy of *The Oxford Times*. Calder had the uncomfortable feeling that the guy was only pretending to read.

Maybe I should just leave, Calder thought to himself. But then, it was such a small town. What if someone ran after him, demanding that he pay for his order? No, the best idea was to stay put and pretend he hadn't noticed a thing. Calder studied his mazes from the graveyard, spreading them out on the table in front of him. He pulled out his pencil and made a couple of minor adjustments.

Several minutes later, he was tapped on the shoulder by something that was definitely not a hand. A wooden cooking spoon hovered by his ear. "Hey!" he said.

"You the bloke with the tuna?" Bird Girl asked. Her voice was mean.

She zipped back behind the counter before he could respond, the spoon now tucked into her apron. "I didn't hear my name," Calder said.

"You wish," she hissed, her voice barely audible. Or had he misunderstood — was that *sand-wish*? Again, he had the distinct feeling that the people around him were waiting — waiting and watching.

He walked over to the counter to pick up his lunch and pay. Bird Girl looked everywhere but at him, slapped down his change on a paper napkin, and shoved it roughly in his direction. Under the coins was scrawled, in red pen, *Real name?* The question mark was big and had a maze-like curl.

"Huh? Mine?" Calder said aloud as he pocketed the change. Before he could answer, the girl swept the napkin into a trash bin under the counter and flew back into the kitchen.

Calder felt the floor shaking as someone walked heavily across the room behind him. His heart began to pound as he wondered what Angry Man was going to do. Would he pulverize Calder for speaking with his daughter? To his great relief, Calder then heard a door slam shut on the side of the room — the man had gone into the bathroom.

Not a moment to lose! Calder pretended to look at his watch, sighed loudly as if he'd forgotten the time, then hurriedly wrapped the sandwich in a wad of napkins and stuffed it into his pocket.

He hurried out the door and down the side-walk, looking back several times. None of the crew was behind him. Had he imagined all of that? What if they thought he'd followed them from the post office and was spying on them? And what had Bird Girl wanted? Did she think he was lying about his name? Or, worse, making a point by using Alexander Calder's name?

He tried the gate to the graveyard, hoping to eat on his tomb, but it was now locked.

Frowning slightly, he headed back toward the town square.

A steady breeze was blowing; large clouds drifted across the blue. Red and yellow leaves swirled overhead, and an occasional ice cream wrapper or stray piece of newspaper flattened against a leg. Two black crows flew side by side, crossing the town on a diagonal.

He passed a grocery store he hadn't noticed before and rattled his leftover lunch money. Oh, good thinking — dessert! Inside, he stood in front of the candy counter and picked up one chocolate bar after another, weighing them carefully. He knew Cadbury was an English chocolate company, because his grandma Ranjana had always loved it and sometimes asked his parents to look for it in Chicago. *Twirl . . . Double Decker . . . Time Out . . . Crunchie . . . Fruit and Nut Bar . . . Dairy Milk Bar . . . Dream.* Calder picked out three: a Twirl, in honor of Tommy ("The Intense Chocolate Hit"), a Dream for Petra, who would love that name, and a Crunchie for his mom, who liked everything crisp.

Rounding the corner before the town square, he was happy to see a familiar blast of red. The sculpture was beginning to feel like his only friend today. He'd sit on a bench. At least in such a public spot there could be no secrets; no one could stuff him in a bag or hang him up.

He sat down, unwrapped his sandwich, and took a huge bite.

"*Yeow!*" said a loud voice.

"Pummy!" Calder exclaimed, thrilled to have the company. When he broke off a chunk of sandwich and held it up, he saw only a black blur and then the quick flash of red mouth, sharp teeth, and one yellow eye. Pummy snatched the bite from his hand and dragged it beneath a neighboring bench, purring loudly.

Calder then thought of Bird Girl sitting here the afternoon before, and of the paper that her father had snatched from her. No one had ever done anything like that with his work. His work!

Suddenly, Calder remembered — he'd left his mazes lying on the table in the Lyon Tea Shop.

CHAPTER FOURTEEN

▲ ▲ ▲ "These yours?" a voice asked moments later in an American accent. It was the man with the sunglasses and the leather jacket.

His mouth full, Calder nodded at the papers being held out to him. "Thanks so much," he managed to say.

"They look like something you wouldn't want to lose. Is it a game?" the man asked.

"They're pentomino mazes," Calder said stiffly, hoping the man would then stop talking. It didn't seem smart to be seen speaking with another American, not now. He looked away, as if the conversation were finished.

Black Jacket sat down on the bench above Pummy, who didn't move. The newspaper opened again, and for a few minutes Calder ate his sandwich, Pummy washed his whiskers, and the man read. Every once in a while the man glanced around, as if waiting for someone else to show up, then disappeared back into his newspaper.

Calder, relieved that neither the man nor Pummy was paying any attention to him, began to look closely at the sculpture.

It was the same metal as the *Flamingo* sculpture in Chicago and was definitely the same color. Much smaller, this sculpture stood about three feet taller than his dad. It was about as long as his bed at home, and as wide as — as what? Maybe a large cow. Or a bull; something about it felt masculine. It was made up of bendy-looking, stretched triangles, five shapes that came together in a kind of startled but sturdy creature.

Calder then saw a small plaque bolted to the ground on one side, something he hadn't noticed before. MINOTAUR, it read, ALEXANDER CALDER, 1959. Wasn't the Minotaur some kind of man-bull combo that ate people? Calder was hazy on the myth, but he remembered that the Minotaur lived in an impossible maze. Some guy found his way through it with yarn and killed the —

"Minotaur!" he blurted, suddenly delighted. Of course; it was perfect for Woodstock. Perfect for the maze, perfect for this town that specialized in large and fierce creatures. Why, then, was everybody so upset?

"I've been listening to what people in the town have to say about it," Black Jacket announced. He stayed behind his paper; Calder could only see one ear and the top of his head.

"Why?" Calder asked him, curiosity winning over caution.

The newspaper, still open, went up and down in a shrug. "I study art," the man said. "And how it affects people."

"Oh!" Calder sat down on a nearby bench and, pulling out one of his pentominoes, told the man in detail about the excitement in Chicago over the Calder mobiles and about the giant and much-loved *Flamingo, Flying Dragon,* and *Universe.* The newspaper came down, and the man smiled. He looked pleased, but not at all surprised. He listened and nodded, but continued to glance around. Suddenly, as if he'd forgotten to do it before, he took off his jacket.

Calder's mouth fell open. "It's the T-shirt, the one from the Chicago exhibit!" he said. "Cool, I thought the shapes looked like parts of a code when I first saw it." Now the black shirt with its row of red Calder sculptures just looked kind of shocking.

"Odd how human history and a sense of what things are *supposed* to look like in a certain place can influence how you actually see," the man said. "Or what you allow yourself to see."

"Exactly! My dad and I — we were so surprised when we first saw this huge red thing in the middle of Woodstock. Actually, I think we were disappointed even though we both love Calder's sculptures. And, now I'm getting used to seeing it here, I kind of like that it gives a person a jolt."

"But you're American. Americans don't worry about tradition, not like older cultures do. Plus, you've seen lots of Alexander Calder's work. There isn't that much of it in England, and this must be the only public Calder piece in the Cotswolds. I've heard mixed reviews coming from the people in this town," the man said. "That's putting it kindly."

"I know . . . but wasn't it a gift?" Calder asked. "Pretty generous. If someone gave this to my neighborhood at home, everyone would be jumping up and down."

The man smiled and shrugged. He looked at the sky, and then at Pummy, who was now snoring. "But that's Chicago. What happens if a gift like this isn't understood or wanted? I can see it's caused some real agony here in Woodstock. What I mean is, perhaps they don't want something modern in a thousand-some-year-old place, or the attention it will bring."

"But tourists come to see Blenheim Palace year-round," Calder said. "How is that different?"

"Blenheim belongs," the man said.

Calder was stirring his pentominoes. "So why doesn't the collector take the Calder back?" he said slowly.

The man folded the paper into a tidy rectangle. "I don't know what will happen. I'm only here to observe," he said, reaching down to scratch Pummy's one visible ear. Pummy didn't move.

"Who —" Calder began, but then realized that he couldn't ask who had hired Black Jacket to watch the art. "How long does it take to belong?" Calder asked instead.

The man glanced around again. "Perhaps too long," he said. "But let's talk about something else. Those diagrams — can you explain them to me? I'm interested."

Black Jacket pulled off his sunglasses, and Calder noticed that his eyes were blue and kind of wandery, like Miss Knowsley's. At that moment, he half turned on the bench, eyes following a large, empty cart pulled by a Clydesdale horse, the kind with massive shoulders and hairy ankles and hooves. He now sat straighter, smiled, and looked directly at Calder.

"They're challenges," Calder explained, and unfolded his graph paper. He moved, sitting down on the bench next to the man. Soon the yellow pentominoes were out of Calder's pocket, and the man and the boy were bent over Calder's diagrams, talking busily. Both waved their hands excitedly and spoke at the same time.

An outsider would never have guessed that they had just met.

▲ ▲ ▲ Looking out the window of his bus an hour later, Walter Pillay spotted his son shaking hands with a man in front of the red Calder sculpture. The huge, black cat lay right nearby. His son was smiling; the man had his back turned. Hmm, at home with the locals already, Calder's dad thought, then sighed as he picked up his briefcase.

Walking toward the door of the bus, he saw a flash, something reflecting from a second-floor window. What was that?

He followed the flash to a camera, and behind the camera was the girl who'd been taking pictures the night before. This time, he realized, she was photographing his son and the man he was talking with, in addition to the red sculpture. How odd. Perhaps that was as close as she was allowed to get.

Well, Calder would be immortalized in

some girl's Woodstock photo collection, Walter Pillay thought to himself and smiled. His son was certainly finding his place here.

Realizing that Calder was growing up, Walter Pillay felt a momentary twinge of sadness.

CHAPTER FIFTEEN

∧ ∧ ∧ The next morning at breakfast, Pummy was nowhere to be seen. Calder wriggled so much in his chair that Miss Knowsley frowned.

"He's going to the maze and Blenheim today," Calder's dad said, not wanting her to think that Calder had a bathroom issue. "A bit excited," he added.

"A bit!" Calder said. "That's an understatement."

Miss Knowsley laughed. "Well, at least the Minotaur is here in the square and not in the middle of the maze," she said briskly. "No worries there."

Walter Pillay looked at his son, wanting to exchange a glance, but Calder looked away. *Slam-slam* went Pummy's door in the kitchen.

"Oh, Pummy dear!" Miss Knowsley called in a chirpy tone. "Come to Mummy-Mums!"

Pummy rolled into the room, ignored Miss Knowsley, squinted directly at Calder, then gave one loud *yeow* and headed up the stairs. Miss Knowsley looked oddly crushed.

"Someone's been leaving food for him again," she said, her voice suddenly angry. "I do hate that! One never knows what the poor dear is trying to digest." She clattered the breakfast dishes into a pile.

Calder swallowed loudly, then busily retied his sneaker laces.

As they shut the front door and stepped outside, both Calder and his dad took a deep breath. The street was quiet, and the air smelled sweet and damp. A window closed softly nearby. "Such a clean and cozy little world," Walter Pillay remarked happily as they headed down Alehouse Lane. "The problems of an overfed cat and a surprising piece of modern art! I wish life in Chicago were that simple."

"I wish," echoed his son with a little smile.

In the distance, Calder spotted Black Jacket — he was walking rapidly down one of the twisty streets that led toward the edge of town. For some reason, and Calder wasn't sure why, he hadn't told his dad the details of the conversation yesterday in the square. Or about what had happened in the post office and the Lyon Tea Shop. Maybe because it was his own adventure. He figured that as you got older — and he would be thirteen this December — you didn't need to share everything.

If Calder and his dad had walked by just seconds later, he would have seen something that might have changed his mind: Angry Dad stepped out of a doorway, and he and Black Jacket shook hands. But as it was, Calder never knew.

And Walter Pillay, for some reason, hadn't mentioned the girl photographing the *Minotaur* from a second-story window. Perhaps he didn't want his son to think he'd been spying on him.

Five minutes later, Walter Pillay waved out the bus window. Calder waved back as he hurried away.

Heading off to get safely lost, Calder's dad thought to himself with a smile. How restful to be staying in a world where that was possible.

▲ ▲ ▲ As the bus drove in one direction and Calder walked in another, the boy was watched by three sets of eyes. One peered from behind a lace window curtain, another through a gate, and the third from behind the steering wheel of a parked truck.

A fourth person studied one of the watchers and muttered softly, "Nothing to it! And they'll never figure it out."

CHAPTER SIXTEEN

▲ ▲ ▲ When Walter Pillay got off the bus that afternoon at five-thirty, Calder was not there. Knowing his son had lots to explore at Blenheim, he wasn't concerned. He walked slowly back to Miss Knowsley's house, enjoying the breeze, and marveled at the continued existence of this old stone community in a modern world. He was pleased that Calder was getting a sense of what it was like to stay in a place that had been lived in for so long; the experience of slow and visible time was just not a part of growing up in the United States.

He rang the bell, since Calder had the key. Miss Knowsley opened the door.

"Left you a note, your boy did," she said briskly.

"Oh," Walter Pillay said, surprised. "Where is it?"

"Dashed upstairs with it," she said, as if the dashing part hadn't been good.

Walter Pillay felt a tiny jab of worry as he

climbed the stairs to their room. The door was closed but unlocked. He sank down on the bed and picked up the piece of graph paper left on his pillow.

Dear Dad,
I've been asked to do some speshal work over at Blenem Palace. I'll be back later, don't wate up.

Love Calder

Walter Pillay read through the note three times. He was used to Calder's exotic spelling. But who had invited him to do something at Blenheim? A kid he'd just met today? And why stay out so late? Hurrying downstairs, he knocked on the kitchen door.

"Come in!" Miss Knowsley and Pummy were both seated on stools at the kitchen table. Miss Knowsley had a chop, a piece of fried bread, and green beans. Pummy had an empty plate.

"He's waiting for his bits," Miss Knowsley said fondly, giving Pummy a nod.

Walter Pillay showed her the note. "Did you notice my son with anyone today?" he asked. She frowned at the piece of paper. Suddenly aware of the spelling, Walter Pillay snatched it back; this was not the moment for another critical comment about Americans.

Miss Knowsley smoothed her apron and squinted her eyes. "No-o-o, I don't think so," she said slowly.

"Is it likely that my son would have been invited to do something at Blenheim? By someone who lives or works there?"

"Hmm, possible." Miss Knowsley glanced at her chop and straightened her glasses. "It's the end of the season over there, you know. Things get less formal. They're used to kids — lots of educational programs. And of course many people work and live on the estate, as you can imagine. Might be a family over there; I'm not entirely sure."

"Fine, thanks. If Calder returns before I do, please keep him here," Walter Pillay said, turning away.

The front door shut with a slam, and Miss

Knowsley put three little pieces of pork on Pummy's plate. "That's my boy. For a job well done," she said lightly.

▲ ▲ ▲ "The grounds remain open until six-thirty this evening," the guard at the Triumphal Arch, the closest gate to Blenheim Park, told a distracted-looking man. "It's just gone six — no need to pay now."

"And if someone wants to leave after the gates are closed?" the man asked.

"Oh, there's always a groundskeeper to let them out," the guard replied.

The man arrived breathless at the palace. The grounds were deserted except for the occasional dog-walker. He circled the building, which was closed for the night, and rang several bells. No one answered, although he could see lights in one wing.

He ran back to the gate, arriving just as the guard was locking his cash box for the day. "Is there any other place —" the man gasped "— where people live on the estate?"

"Besides the family?" the guard asked cheerfully. "Many places. Cottages and lodges, some for guests, some for help." He waved his hand toward the woods and gardens and lake that stretched as far as the eye could see. "Tucked here and there," he added.

Walter Pillay explained that he was looking for his son, who had left him a note. The man threw back his head and laughed. "And you're American, is that right?"

Walter Pillay nodded.

"No need for worry, no need at all," the guard said and patted him on the back. "No crime around here, not like the United States. Your son is most probably having a visit with one of the gardeners, and will be walked to the gate in an hour or so. Go by one of our nice little pubs and have yourself a pint. He'll turn up in no time!"

Walter Pillay walked slowly back through the streets. He would have given a lot, at that moment, to hear the clatter-clatter of Calder's pentominoes. He reminded himself that his son was

used to navigating Hyde Park and parts of downtown Chicago on his own. He'd done it for years. And Chicago, after all, was the third-largest city in the United States. In comparison, Woodstock was like someone's backyard; Calder would show up any second.

Calder's dad turned down one empty street after another. Almost everyone in town must have been inside cooking or eating. At this hour, the buildings looked unfriendly, like small castles, and the unkempt graveyards seemed downright spooky. A cold wind was blowing, whooshing across the Calder sculpture, through church spires and trees, over ancient walls and around iron gates. Once the sun set, color drained from the streets and all was suddenly hard: stone, metal, stone, stone, stone. Old wasn't always cozy, he noted to himself.

What on earth could Calder, a twelve-year-old boy, have been invited to do at Blenheim? And by whom? Something didn't feel right.

Walter Pillay shook his head, trying to clear the thickening fog of worries.

CHAPTER SEVENTEEN

▲ ▲ ▲ He jerked awake at dawn, still dressed. A package of biscuits was crushed under one elbow, and the tea he had heated on the electric burner in the room was still on the table. He must have fallen asleep — and Calder! — he twisted around in the chair, ready to see Calder's black hair sticking out in all directions on the pillow.

Calder's bed was still empty.

Walter Pillay stood so quickly that he saw black for a moment, and then yellow spots. His heart was pounding. As his vision cleared, he heard a shout from the street: "It's gone! The sculpture is gone!"

▲ ▲ ▲ In no time at all, the streets had filled with police cars. The town square was outlined with wooden barriers. A police photographer worked busily, documenting every inch of the crime area. A number of townspeople had come out with their cameras, and now stood on benches or flower urns and snapped pictures, their cameras held high over their heads. Walter Pillay noticed the young girl from the day before yesterday, also taking photos. This time she didn't look as furtive. Perhaps her father was away at work, or perhaps it was simply that other people were taking pictures, too. There was something yellow on the pavement where the sculpture had been, and a number of officers stood around it, talking. Walter Pillay ran over, his hair ruffled and his shirt untucked. He spoke with the closest man in uniform, describing his missing son and the note.

The man frowned suddenly. He brought Calder's dad inside the barriers and showed him what the police were looking at.

Walter Pillay's stomach lurched. The words were cleanly stenciled in yellow paint, each letter about five inches high:

WISH

"Don't know what to make of this," the detective said. "A bit like the work of Banksy. Of

course, no one knows what Banksy looks like, he keeps his identity a secret, and I must say I've never heard of him stealing. He's more of a prankster, someone who likes to raise questions about art."

The detective sounded excited by the idea, and kept glancing around as if Banksy were watching. "Might be taking pictures of what he's stirred up," the detective went on. "Does it all the time. Could be anywhere. Could have hired one of these locals."

Walter Pillay had heard of the British artist Banksy, but was barely listening. The words *prankster* and *likes to raise questions* sparked a new set of worries. Two Calders gone in one day — was there a connection? Had his son been manipulated into helping with someone else's joke? Or with a crime he didn't realize was a crime?

His heart heavy, he went back to the bed-and-breakfast and telephoned Calder's mom. She burst into tears as they tried to reassure each other. The plan was for her to book a flight for London as soon as possible. If Calder showed up in the next hour or two, she would cancel her trip; otherwise, she'd be there by late that night. Meanwhile, she got busy e-mailing an image of Calder to her husband, an image that he could show the police.

Miss Knowsley hurried out of her house an hour later. By then, Walter Pillay was walking through the grounds of Blenheim with two detectives, looking for any trace of his son and speaking with each of the groundskeepers who had been on duty the day before.

When Calder's dad saw Miss Knowsley trotting toward him, her apron flapping, he hurried over. No, not good news: It was an emergency phone call from his wife. Walter Pillay ran all the way back to the bed-and-breakfast and called her from the phone in the dining room. After hanging up, he sank down in a chair, his head in his hands. Yvette Pillay had tripped over her suitcase and fallen down the front steps of their house, landing on her back on the cement walk. She couldn't move without great pain, and had been taken to the hospital.

Tears filled Walter Pillay's eyes, something that hadn't happened since his mother, Ranjana, had died a few years before. Calder had seemingly vanished. Yvette was now injured. This father-son visit to England had spun overnight into a nightmare. He hung up the phone and sat for a moment in the front breakfast room, trying to think.

Calder, Calder, Calder . . . he knew his son inside out, but had to admit to himself that these days he didn't always know what kinds of projects Calder was involved in until after the fact. Petra Andalee and Tommy Segovia, as his best friends, might know. The three of them had done some extraordinary detective work on their own in Hyde Park, some of it quite dangerous. And none of their parents, amazingly, had guessed or understood the seriousness of their investigations until they were over. Petra and Tommy certainly knew how Calder thought.

Walter Pillay picked up one of the balls of wool in the basket and rolled it back and forth between his palms. Then he dropped the wool and reached for the phone again. It was worth a try.

The floors in the house slanted in every conceivable direction, and the red ball rolled unnoticed out into the front hall, where it stopped by Pummy's collar.

"*Yeow.*" Pummy opened his yellow eye and batted at the ball. A loose strand caught on his collar buckle, and he pulled angrily at it. When he got up to leave minutes later, the yarn trailed behind him. The entire ball, still unrolling, shot out through the cat door in the kitchen.

⋀ ⋀ ⋀ That morning, the police learned nothing about where the Calder sculpture had gone. The welded steel structure could, they admitted, have been lifted by five or six strong men onto a cart with rubber tires, the kind used on market day in the town square. A number of those carts, owned by the town and available to local farmers, stood in a field outside the walls to Blenheim, and no one could agree on exactly how many were usually available. One could be missing. There were always clots of earth and boot prints in town, so that was no help. And in the area around where the sculpture had stood, there were no streaks of paint indicating that the *Minotaur* had been scraped or dragged. No one had heard any disturbances during the night. The locals seemed quite cheerful about losing their work of art, and asked few questions.

The post office that morning was a-buzz with jokes and comments:

"Looks like the *Minotaur* went a-hunting!"

"Got to be careful what you wish for . . ."

"Yup, hungry and bored."

"Maybe those legs got loosened up, and the thing ran off!"

"But *tsk*, *tsk*, the boy. Have you seen his dad? Worried to pieces, he is."

"The kid'll turn up by noon, probably just run off on an overnight scoot. This isn't a minotaur that's likely to eat him — other way around, if I know boys that age. Ravenous, that's what he'll be. When I was that age, I wandered off to . . ."

▲ ▲ ▲ Woodstock was particularly chatty that morning, but only when the police were busy elsewhere. No one in uniform was surprised — village life in England had never depended entirely on the law.

Two kinds of fliers were printed up and posted around town. Calder's face appeared on one, with the words, MISSING: CALDER PILLAY, AMERICAN CITIZEN, AGED 12, LAST SEEN IN BLENHEIM PARK.

The other had a photograph of the *Minotaur*, with the words, STOLEN: SCULPTURE BY ALEXANDER CALDER. LAST SEEN IN MARKET SQUARE, WOODSTOCK.

All morning the police listened and questioned and tromped through the grounds at Blenheim. The Marlborough family, the 11th Duke and his wife, were away and couldn't be reached. No guests were staying in lodges or cottages. Fifteen workers, however, lived in apartments above garages and behind barns on the property, which included far more land than was open to the public. All of these employees were questioned by the police.

One gardener had driven by Calder standing alone on the bridge, peering over the side. Another had seen him running into the old walled Kitchen Garden area, probably headed for the maze. Another had seen him walking in the fountains behind the palace. No one had seen him enter a building. No one had seen him speak with anyone.

Two officers were ordered to walk through every path inside the maze. They had been told that the boy carried a set of yellow plastic puzzle pieces in his pocket; Calder's dad had drawn pictures of the twelve pentominoes for the police. Maze maps in hand, they agreed to divide the acre, and set out in different directions. Both got lost and passed each other again and again, unable to relate the map to the dizzying channels of green.

In the embarrassment of not knowing where

they were, neither officer spotted a small yellow L, a flat piece of plastic shaped like a boot, sticking out beneath one of the hedges. It was flanked by a Red Hots candy box and a blue ball, the kind used for jacks. There was a fair amount of this-and-that garbage under the bushes; kids were always dropping things. When the maze was closed at the end of the season, every inch of the ground was raked clean. Until then, toys and bits of paper drifted and got buried under leaves or mud.

The fact that the artist's last name and the boy's first name were the same was certainly irritating. The police hoped the boy would turn up shortly, having gotten tired of his adventure or joke or whatever silliness this was, and they could get down to the real business of figuring out who had stolen the sculpture. Although Walter Pillay had given the police the note Calder had written to him, no one who had noticed the boy in town remembered seeing him make friends with anyone. Oddly, Walter Pillay and the mysterious girl in the window seemed to be the only ones who had seen Calder shaking hands with an adult near the sculpture. How was this possible, in the main town square?

When Calder's dad told the police about the girl with the camera and pointed to the window, they nodded and frowned. Unfortunately, the window belonged to a clothing store; anyone could have been looking out.

Meanwhile, the police referred to The Boy and The Artist, dropping the name Calder entirely.

CHAPTER EIGHTEEN

▲ ▲ ▲ Neither Petra nor Tommy had left the United States before, and Mrs. Sharpe hadn't left for over twenty years. Getting the three of them overnight passports, tickets, and enough clean clothing was a sizable job.

Before Petra and Tommy could truly absorb the news that Calder had vanished and that they were going to England to look for him, they were on the plane, side by side, Mrs. Sharpe across the aisle. It was not a situation that Petra, Tommy, or Mrs. Sharpe had ever imagined.

Both kids had been horrified when they'd first heard the news about Calder. Petra immediately thought about how dreamy her good friend could be when he was busy thinking through an important pentomino idea, and Tommy thought about how his old buddy didn't always know what to say to strangers or when to run. They had to believe that Calder had probably decided to take on a project, some kind of rescue mission. While Tommy and Petra didn't always understand each other, both were sure they understood Calder. They would find him.

The trip had been Mrs. Sharpe's idea. When the calls to Petra and Tommy came through from Walter Pillay, who asked if they had any thoughts about what his son might be up to, they immediately told their old teacher Ms. Hussey, who then called her elderly Hyde Park friend. Mrs. Sharpe had met the three kids during a couple of earlier adventures; they had been to her house for tea, and she had helped them with some detective work. She liked their determination and enjoyed their company — in small doses.

An hour after Ms. Hussey called, Mrs. Sharpe called Yvette Pillay, who had cracked a disk in her spine and was unable to travel, and then Walter Pillay. Next came Petra's parents, Frank and Norma Andalee, and Tommy's mom, Zelda Segovia. As Mrs. Sharpe put it, she could afford to fund the expedition for all three of them, she was familiar with the kids, and she wouldn't put up with any nonsense. She was the perfect chaperone.

Everyone agreed: Bringing Calder's best friends to Woodstock to help the police figure out where he might be was not only sensible, it was the only thing to do.

Walter Pillay was pleased they were coming, but worried about something else. He had gotten a call from Ms. Hussey.

She told him what she had whispered to Calder that day in her classroom: "Play the Calder Game in England! And don't tell anyone what you're doing."

She now felt guilty.

"But I said *Calder Game*," Ms. Hussey had repeated. "Nothing else."

"Yes, but don't forget we're talking about two Calders here," Walter Pillay had said quietly. "And that immediately means a number of games."

"Yes," Ms. Hussey had murmured. "Oh, dear."

CHAPTER NINETEEN

▲ ▲ ▲ Tommy had his elbow on the armrest, and was wolfing down his macaroni and cheese. He choked, and a chunk of noodle shot sideways and landed on the cover of Petra's notebook.

"*Eeuw*, Tommy! Watch it!" Petra took her napkin and carefully captured the noodle. She had only picked at her food, and was trying to write while Tommy ate. He made such disgusting chewing sounds that it was hard to concentrate. They hadn't spent any time together since Calder had left, and now Petra remembered why.

Tommy looked at her, shrugged, and moved on to the butterscotch pudding. By the time he'd finished, Petra had read the same question about five times:

> Is there a game that makes a player seem to disappear even if he or she is not really gone?

She put down her pen and closed her eyes. There was hide and seek, of course, and the hedge maze. But what about a more complicated game? She had no idea.

Maybe a mobile would help. She flipped to the back of her notebook, which had many pages of mobile-poems. She drew some lines. Then she added words, slowly, one at a time.

Tommy glanced sideways and saw:

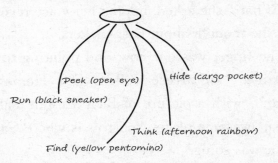

Weird, he thought to himself. It looked like a jellyfish with tentacles. He understood it, though — Calder liked all of the things Petra had written down, and they were looking for Calder.

The next thing Petra knew, Tommy was wrestling a magazine out of the seat-back pocket in front of him, tearing several pages. His elbow jabbed Petra in the side as he settled back into his seat. She scrunched herself as far away from him as possible. He didn't seem to notice. He was busily rubbing his first finger, which was not clean, back forth under his nose as he turned the pages. At least it was *under*, she thought to herself, and not *in*.

"Petra!" Tommy squealed suddenly. The finger disappeared into his nose.

"What?" she asked, hoping her voice revealed what she thought about nose-pickers.

The finger was out now, and pointing to the magazine. "An article called 'Old Homes in England,' with a picture of Blen-hee-ime Palace! Whoa, awesome place! And this is where Calder said he was going."

Despite herself, Petra leaned over to see. "It's pronounced Blen-em — you don't pay attention to the 'h' or 'i.'"

"Whatever. I know."

Petra now wished she hadn't corrected him; she didn't like kids who thought they knew everything. "Whatever," she agreed.

The two studied the spread of pictures in front of them. They saw a lake, a river, lawns and gardens that looked larger than their entire neighborhood in Chicago, and a stone house with two-story columns and about a million windows. It was easily the largest house either one had ever seen.

Tommy said aloud what Petra was already thinking: "I can't imagine Calder in this fancy place. Who could have invited him to do something there? This is too weird!"

Mrs. Sharpe looked across the aisle. "Stranger things have happened on that piece of land."

Couldn't be much stranger than being on this trip with you, Tommy thought to himself. He knew Mrs. Sharpe was a good person, but she was frightening. The way she spoke, you felt as if you'd done something wrong even if you hadn't.

Petra leaned across Tommy. "What kinds of things?" she asked. "I read *Alice's Adventures in Wonderland*, and I know Lewis Carroll lived nearby in Oxford, but that's about it. I was going to look for a book on Woodstock —"

"No need, I have one." Mrs. Sharpe held up a thin, crimson volume with a tattered cover.

Her voice didn't sound like she wanted to lend the book.

"Can you tell us a few things?" Petra repeated. Tommy sucked in his cheeks and glanced admiringly at her. She was brave, no doubt about it.

Mrs. Sharpe picked a thread off her skirt. Tommy was relieved to see she wasn't angry, and watched her gold bracelet disappear into the loose skin that had bunched up on her wrist; the woman was as skinny as a toothpick.

"Maybe." She straightened her reading glasses and opened the book again. "The Romans lived on this land, several thousand years ago. Remains of large country houses, or villas, have been excavated on the property, and they've found a Roman road, now called Akeman Street, in Blenheim Park. Yes . . . the 'Chase' at Woodstock meant the 'Park,' and the name Woodstock itself means a stockaded settlement buried in trees —"

"Like the stockade in *Treasure Island*!" Tommy blurted, proud that he could contribute something from a book. He wasn't much of a reader.

When Mrs. Sharpe didn't respond or even look up, Petra mouthed *Right* to Tommy. She knew Mrs. Sharpe wasn't big on other people's feelings.

"— and most of Oxfordshire was forest, deep forest. In addition to the wooded area known as Woodstock, there was Wychwood, Cornbury, Stowood, and Shotover. The Saxons took over after the Romans, in the fifth century, and the Anglo-Saxons lived and hunted in the area for many hundreds of years. Then came the Norman Conquest, and a manor house was built at Woodstock by Henry II, one of the first Norman kings. That was, oh, 1125 or so. It sat on a hill by the River Glyme, which is the river that still flows into Blenheim Park."

Tommy's mind was wandering, but he heard the place names: *chase*, *ache*-man, *witch*-wood, *shot*-over, *glyme*, which sounded just like slime. The place would be spooky, no doubt about it. And the possibilities for an expert scavenger like himself! Imagine several thousand years of things dropped or lost in the dirt. Tommy wriggled with excitement, picturing himself digging up ancient treasure. Maybe that was what Calder was already doing.

Tommy slipped his hand into his pocket, fingering the blue button he'd never returned to Ms. Button. He'd been waiting for just the right dramatic moment in school to make it reappear, but then had decided yesterday to bring it with him. Who could tell — perhaps it would work as a trophy, a reminder of how capable he was as a finder. Perhaps it would bring good luck.

Mrs. Sharpe cleared her throat. "So King Henry II had his hunting lodge by the side of the lake, across from what is now Blenheim Palace. Hmm, he had a mistress, Rosamund Clifford, who lived in her own house nearby, apparently protected by a complicated maze that the king built. It was described hundreds of years later as having 'strange winding walls and turnings.' There's a story that Queen Eleanor of Aquitaine, Henry's wife, traveled secretly to Woodstock and followed a piece of yarn attached to his spur as he entered the maze. She supposedly found him with Rosamund and offered her rival either poison or a knife, and Rosamund chose the poison — although other accounts say Henry's mistress lived to be quite old in a nunnery nearby. There is still a well where the house stood, called Rosamund's Well, although the old lodge and maze are now gone."

Petra elbowed Tommy. *Maze*, she mouthed, her eyebrows going up.

Murder, he mouthed back, then frowned. Murder inside a maze was not a happy thought.

Mrs. Sharpe looked over. "The laws about hunting on royal land became ferocious with the English kings. People were cruelly punished for disobeying. The distance between the rich and the poor was huge. By the 1200s, there were 137 houses of some kind in the area that is now the old town of Woodstock, where we'll be staying. These were people who served the monarchy's needs, and their last names usually said what they did — Henry le Yronmongare, someone who worked with iron, and John le Deyere, a man who worked with dyes, or John le Wymplere, someone who made wimples, which were hats that the medieval women wore."

Petra giggled. Mrs. Sharpe looked at her as if to say, I didn't think *you* would laugh about this.

"Just thinking: Calder the Math Whiz, Tommy the Finder, Petra the Scribbler. And you, Mrs. Sharpe —" Petra paused. "Maybe you had relatives who worked with sharp tools or something. I mean . . ."

"Yes, how fitting," Mrs. Sharpe said, and almost smiled.

She touched the corner of her mouth with her little finger, as if removing a crumb, and continued brusquely: "Lots of murder and quarreling on this land. Hmm, yes, people hung and poisoned . . . and Elizabeth Tudor, great-umpteenth grandmother of the current Queen Elizabeth, was imprisoned at Woodstock in the 1500s for several months, before she came to the throne. Later, the land was given to John Churchill, the first Duke of Marlborough, by Queen Anne, as a thank-you for winning a big battle against Louis XIV in Europe. This was a giant honor, to be given land that had been used by English kings and queens for over six centuries. Like giving away a piece of the heart of England.

"Blenheim Palace was built between 1705 and 1722, and each of the various dukes added something to the property. Let's see . . . the high stone wall of Woodstock Park is thought to have been the first park wall in England, and it was already old when the first duke took over. It runs for such a distance that it took over thirty years to repair it.

"Here's something quite extraordinary: The fourth duke added a waterfall now known as the Grand Cascade, in the 1760s. In order to impress his guests, he installed a surprise. He'd stroll with them along the bank above the falls until they reached a huge boulder in the middle of the path, a boulder blocking their view. As his visitors murmured their disappointment, the duke would step forward and press a hidden lever or spring. Magically, the boulder then rumbled to one side and the group found themselves stepping onto a protected platform next to the water. From there, guests could admire the view and also keep their fancy clothes dry. Predictably, that didn't last. The falls have tumbled into a more natural state."

"Sounds pretty modern," murmured Petra.

Tommy nodded.

Mrs. Sharpe paused, yawned daintily through an almost-closed mouth, and without even a glance at Petra and Tommy to see if they wanted to hear more, continued, "Each one of the dukes has added to the hundreds of acres of formal gardens, and the ninth duke planted almost half a million trees. Winston Churchill, the great leader in World War II, was a member of the family and was born at Blenheim in 1874. Several wings of the palace and some of the grounds were opened to the public in the mid-twentieth century to help pay for the costs of keeping such a massive piece of property. Gracious, it's 11,400 acres."

Mrs. Sharpe read on to herself, and seemed to have forgotten about Petra and Tommy.

"Amazing, the idea of a family living in one place for so many generations," Petra said after several moments of quiet.

"Petra?" Tommy's voice was low. "Do you really think Calder's okay?"

"We talked about it at home — of course I do! We'll find him. He's probably on an investigation that's important, and just doesn't realize all the adults are worried."

"All those gruesome names, and that bloody history . . ." Tommy mumbled, picking some black dirt from under his fingernail.

"Just remember the Button. I'm sure he decided to have a fantastic adventure because of what we have to live with at school this year. Hey, isn't that the perfect name for her? Her relatives made buttons, and now she *is* one!"

They giggled, and Tommy pulled the large, blue button out of his pocket. Petra looked delighted and gave him a thumbs-up, but as they settled down in their seats, both seemed troubled — more so than they had at the beginning of the trip. The hugeness of going across the Atlantic Ocean to England, to a strange and once-violent place where Calder had vanished, was beginning to sink in.

CHAPTER TWENTY

▲ ▲ ▲ Mrs. Sharpe had hired a car to take them all from the airport to Woodstock. The drive was long and slippery. Petra was in the middle of an ice-smooth backseat, and busy trying not to touch either Mrs. Sharpe or Tommy with any part of her body.

It was hard to see out, and she had to look through the front windshield, which was small. England was green, even in the fall, and had curving hills in every direction and stone walls bordering almost every road. Chicago was flat, and the only stone walls were concrete dividers in highways; Petra was fascinated by the up-and-down feeling of driving in this country, and the homemade look of things. The highway was narrow in some places and wide in others, and ducked through the middle of twisty towns.

"Whee, it's a roller coaster! Too bad we're not speeding —" Tommy stopped, having glanced over at Mrs. Sharpe.

"Yes, too bad we're not dead," she snapped, and gazed brightly out the window as if she had only commented on the weather.

Tommy slouched. Petra hardly dared to breathe. It was a relief when they saw the signs for Woodstock.

As they were unloading the car, Tommy said, "Awesome!" in a delighted voice and promptly dragged his suitcase right over Mrs. Sharpe's toe. He didn't even look down when he felt the bump — assuming it was a cobblestone, he pulled harder once his suitcase stopped moving. In Hyde Park, Mrs. Sharpe wore thick shoes with laces, but for traveling she had put on something closer to a leather glove, a glove with a large silver buckle on the front. She yelped in agony and, before Tommy could apologize, whacked him on the leg with her walking stick.

He froze, mouth open, shocked that she'd hit him. It was so sudden and awkward that Petra was dying to laugh, tried hard not to, and then snorted explosively, sounding more like a large mammal than a girl. As she dug madly for a tissue and Tommy made outraged faces, Mrs. Sharpe marched ahead into the guesthouse. The words "brats," "bad idea," and "manners" drifted out across the English afternoon.

Miss Knowsley only had visitors stay in one room of her house on Alehouse Lane, and that was the one Walter Pillay had rented. Mrs. Sharpe and the kids were five minutes away, in three rooms above a tea shop near the gate to Blenheim Park. The largest room looked out on a graveyard. Petra's and Tommy's rooms were across the hall and looked out on the street. All three were connected by a thin, uneven hallway that groaned and creaked with every step. Petra had never heard such a noisy floor.

Mrs. Sharpe turned toward the kids before closing her door. "The plan is to meet Walter Pillay for an early dinner in an hour. We'll unpack and rest until then," she ordered.

"But I'd like to start looking," Petra said in her most reasonable voice.

"Yeah," echoed Tommy, rubbing his leg.

Mrs. Sharpe said nothing, turned quietly, and swung the door shut. Petra and Tommy could hear the *thunk-click* of a bolt.

"See you," Petra said to Tommy, then shrugged.

He paused, then nodded.

The kids went into their separate rooms and also closed and locked the doors, feeling both grown-up and a little upset. After all, shouldn't they be out looking for Calder? What if he was in a situation where every minute counted? Did Mrs. Sharpe really expect them to stay alone and inside?

▲ ▲ ▲ *"Pssst!"*

Petra looked up from her notebook — something was moving outside her window. A bent piece of black wire with a square of paper speared on the end of it bobbed up and down.

"Pssst!" she heard again.

She hurried over, opened her window as wide

as it would go, and grabbed the folded paper. LOOK OUT NOW, it said. Subtle, she thought to herself a little meanly, noticing at the same time that the stone sill on her window had a big dip in the middle. Was that from people leaning on their elbows and watching the world go by? Time is strange, she thought to herself, imagining many hundreds of elbows over hundreds of years. She looked out.

The end of the clothes hanger was now tangled in Tommy's curtain, and the lace waggled busily around his head. Petra giggled.

Tommy scowled at her. "Cut it out! I'm the one who thought of escaping!"

"*Shh*, whisper! Where to?" Petra asked.

"Just a little exploring."

Both were now leaning on their elbows.

"What about the squeaky boards?" Petra looked doubtful.

"We can walk on the very edges, next to the wall. And if she catches us, we'll explain we needed to get started," Tommy said.

Soon both were creeping down the narrow hallway. Tommy was right. There was almost no sound if they stuck to the sides.

As they stepped onto the sidewalk, Petra held out her hand in a high-five. Tommy gave it a loud smack. This hurt, but she knew he and Calder celebrated with even harder ones. Besides, if she and Tommy couldn't get along, they'd never get anything done.

"Okay, what next?" was all she said, rubbing her hand on the seat of her pants. Then, before Tommy could respond, she gasped.

Across the street, a large crow sat on the curb with a crumpled piece of graph paper in his beak. The paper was a pale blue with black lines; both Tommy and Petra recognized it.

Petra waved her arms, and the crow took off, paper and all. "That was dumb!" Tommy said. "Now we've lost our first clue!"

"I was trying to get the crow to drop it!" Petra was stung. She and Calder never called each other dumb, even when they were mad. "I'm going for my own walk," she said.

"Fine." Tommy turned the other way and headed off.

▲ ▲ ▲ Petra checked her watch: She had just about a half hour before she had to be back in the room. If Tommy was on time, fine. If not, that would be fine, too. He's so impossible, she thought to herself angrily.

Looking for the old town square, Petra walked cautiously around a block shaped like a wedge of pie. It was easy to get confused here; unhurried streets wandered off in all directions, as if going someplace didn't really matter.

The faces around her were bony and seemed to fit with the surrounding stone. People had gray wool sweaters and black or green rubber boots, and almost everybody wore a scarf knotted neatly like a hangman's noose. Petra zipped up her sweatshirt. She felt large and dark and kind of blurry, like a drawing where the color ran over the lines. Maybe this was what visitors to this tidy world always felt like.

She turned another corner and found herself

on the edge of the square. Aha! So this was the area where the Alexander Calder sculpture had stood. She knew that Calder had been talking to a man, right here, on the day he disappeared. Talking and shaking hands.

She walked closer.

Across the crime tape, she saw the yellow stencil:

The Is crossed in a pentomino-like X, and the Ws, with one tipped on its side, spelled *WE*. And then, with *SH-SH*, it read like a warning to be quiet. Was she looking at a compass? A game? Some kind of hint? *Wish . . . Wish.*

She did. She wished with all her heart that Calder would turn up. Suddenly, now that she was here in this unfamiliar place, the idea of

something bad happening to him no longer
seemed far-fetched.

▲ ▲ ▲ "Petra!"

She turned and saw Tommy hurrying toward
her. His mouth was open, and his eyes were perfectly round. "A policeman just grabbed me by
the arm and wanted to see my passport! It's in the
room, so when he turned away to say something
to a grown-up, I ran!"

"Hmm," Petra said, not quite willing to be
friendly.

"Okay, okay," Tommy said. "I'll try not to call
you any more names. I'm wondering how we'll
ever get into Blen-hime — I mean Blen-um —
Park with all these cops around and the entrance
closed off. Have you seen the park walls? They're
gigantic!"

Petra looked at the sky and then at Tommy.
"Maybe we'll wish ourselves in," she said slowly.

Tommy just stared at her. Then he saw the
WISH-WISH.

"Weird," he muttered. "You know what Calder thought about the X piece, that it was the hardest to fit into a pentomino rectangle, so you never leave it until last. Well, here it's in the middle, already in place."

"I wonder what the X-shape means in a maze?" Petra asked. She was aware, suddenly, that someone standing nearby had stepped closer, as if to listen — a pale girl about her age, wearing black clothing. Petra looked at her and the girl spun away, rooting in a large plastic bag as if looking for something.

"One good choice out of four," Tommy said promptly, then grinned. "Hey, pretty good, I'm doing puzzle-thinking like Calder! No, *for* Calder!"

"As long as he's still thinking, too," Petra said.

Tommy scowled up at her chin. What was *that* supposed to mean?

He shrugged, not wanting to ask. Earlier that afternoon, the sun peeking through leaves and between buildings had made cheerful shapes ripple across all this stone. Now the light was cool and flat, and the town looked far less friendly. Suddenly, he missed his mom and his goldfish back in Hyde Park. Goldman always had good ideas — he would have known where to look and what to do.

There isn't any orange here at all, Tommy thought with a shiver. Just beat-up stone, an un-blue sky, blackbirds, two yellow wishes, a missing red sculpture . . . and a missing boy.

Missing boy — Tommy found himself counting the ten letters. Ten horrible letters.

CHAPTER TWENTY-ONE

▲ ▲ ▲ Dinner that night was at a restaurant called The Weasel. Walter Pillay looked as though he'd barely slept over the past two days, and Petra and Tommy were awake but yawning. Mrs. Sharpe did most of the talking.

"Well, there's Pigeon Tart with Leeks, Steak and Guinness Pie, Partridge on Bubble-and-Squeak with Red Onion Marmalade . . ." She didn't seem to notice the lack of enthusiasm.

"Think I'll have the Duck, Blood Pudding, and Mash with a Poached Egg," Petra said tentatively.

"I'll have the Rump Steak with Fat Chips," Tommy said, then gave Petra a poke with his elbow. She shot him a *what's-that-for* look, followed by a *no-don't-tell-me* sigh.

Mrs. Sharpe sniffed and ordered a Jacket Potato and Whipped Squash.

Walter Pillay ordered Beer-Battered Fish, then hardly touched it. Tommy wondered, again, at all the violent language: blood, mash, whipping, even battering, and all attached to food. England was a strange place.

"I walked around Blenheim Park today," Calder's dad began. His face sagged. "I just can't imagine where he could be. I've thought of some kind of rescue mission involving the sculpture, the kind of thing the three of you have gotten into before, but all I can think of is why rescue something that isn't in danger? Plus, it's huge — too heavy to lift and too big to easily hide. And why would Calder have anything to do with valuable art disappearing?"

He sighed. "The locals don't seem too unhappy about the sculpture being gone. I guess they felt it wasn't appropriate, despite the fact that it was a minotaur to go with their maze."

Tommy suddenly sat up. "I forget the exact story, but didn't the Minotaur, ahh . . . eat people?"

"Mmm," mused Walter Pillay, frowning now. "I've been trying not to remember that."

Mrs. Sharpe cleared her throat. "I believe it's

an ancient Greek legend, one of the more gruesome ones. The king of the Greek island of Crete, King Minos, found himself in an unfortunate situation with his queen, who fell in love with a bull. The result was the Minotaur, who was half bull, half man — and liked to eat humans. King Minos built his world-famous maze, where he imprisoned this monster and fed him every so often with young men and women."

Petra glanced at Calder's dad, who had pushed his food away. "Only an old myth," Petra murmured.

"Of course," Mrs. Sharpe said coldly. "At any rate, Theseus found his way into the maze with a ball of yarn or thread, and killed the Minotaur with a sword. The end."

Tommy and Petra looked at their plates. Out of the corner of her eye, Petra saw Mrs. Sharpe place one bony hand on Walter Pillay's arm. "You don't think a Minotaur could stop us from finding your boy, do you?"

Walter Pillay blew his nose.

"He's probably digging up ancient king and queen stuff, and you'll be able to retire when you get back to Hyde Park," Tommy blurted.

"Or he's busy helping with some kind of — well, some kind of large pattern. You know how he recognizes things." Petra's voice trailed off.

Mrs. Sharpe pushed back her chair in a businesslike way. "If you find something old here, you can't always keep it. That's British law. Anyway, it's time we were all in bed. We have a great deal of detective work to do tomorrow." She turned toward Petra and Tommy. "Prepare yourselves, children, to think your way through a real maze. I know you can do it."

Somehow, her bossy tone felt just right. On their way back through the silent streets toward the guesthouse, Tommy noticed with interest that she barely used her cane. Despite the cobblestones and high curbs, she wasn't even looking at the ground, as she usually did in Hyde Park. She peered down every street and in every window.

She was looking for Calder.

"She's already *in* the maze!" Petra whispered to Tommy. Tommy gave her a strange look, and Petra suddenly missed Calder more than ever. Calder would have understood what she meant.

"I am indeed," Mrs. Sharpe said. "And you should both know that my hearing is excellent."

The rest of the walk was silent.

▲ ▲ ▲ On their way up the stairs, Petra and Tommy signaled to each other behind Mrs. Sharpe's back, intending to at least open their doors and have a last whisper in the hallway. But that didn't happen. Within minutes, both were dead asleep.

Out in the old market square, the night rolled on, a moon crept in and out of clouds, and the yellow painted words, WISH-WISH, twinkled in the dark.

At midnight a pair of feet in rubber boots walked softly across the letters. The boots were followed, at a distance of about twenty feet, by a very large cat. Several blocks away, a long piece of red yarn snaked around fences, across the top of a rubbish can, under a delivery truck, and between the stones in a graveyard. It ended in a mucky puddle near the Blenheim Park wall.

Two large and four small, the feet moved on through the night.

CHAPTER TWENTY-TWO

Λ Λ Λ Tommy and Petra both woke fully dressed. Tommy jumped to his feet, horrified that he'd fallen asleep while his buddy Calder was missing someplace in this strange town. Petra also startled awake with a guilty feeling, and immediately began flipping through her notebook to a clean page. She wrote quickly:

> I dreamed I was a word that had gotten tangled inside the Calder Game. I couldn't move, not on my own, and that felt terrible. Whose game was I dreaming about?
>
> Even though I was a word, I was alive but not me. I wonder what I meant.

Someone knocked on her door, a brusque *tat-tat*. She hopped up, forgetting she hadn't washed, changed her clothes, or fixed her hair.

"Oh, my," Mrs. Sharpe said as Petra opened the door a crack. "We'll meet you in the tearoom downstairs." As Petra closed the door, she saw Tommy mouth a panicky *hurry* to her. Being alone with Mrs. Sharpe was not a part of his plan.

Petra hurried into the bathroom, splashed water on her face, and wrestled her hair into a ponytail — there was no time for working on tangles. She yanked on a clean sweatshirt and rushed out the door.

As she slid into her place at the table, knocking one of the table legs and spilling tea, Mrs. Sharpe said calmly, "I have a plan." She paused. "And it's not for the clumsy."

Petra cringed, and Tommy gave her a sympathetic glance. "I mean the local police," Mrs. Sharpe went on. "Do you understand? *They* follow the rules, but *you* might not."

For the first time, Petra began to wonder just how sane Mrs. Sharpe really was.

"We're ready," Tommy said, although Petra thought he didn't sound ready at all. She wished they were with Calder, which would have changed the balance at the table. Calder would just have looked blankly at Mrs. Sharpe, and then she might have explained herself a bit more.

As it was, both kids nodded. Several muffins were eaten in silence.

Finally, Mrs. Sharpe patted her mouth and said, "Well? Off you both go."

"What about your plan?" Tommy asked.

"My plan is to leave the two of you alone. My only demands: You stay together, carry your passports at all times, and be back here at five o'clock on the dot. You'll do far better on your own."

She handed each of them an envelope and said only, "Use this."

She stood, buttoned up her coat, and hobbled out the door, heading in the direction of the main square.

"Awesome," Tommy said.

"Quite a vote of confidence," Petra added, sounding doubtful.

Tommy already had his envelope open. Inside were several bills, fastened with a sticky note that said *Lunch*, and a small, printed card.

It read, in elegant cursive letters, *Louise Coffin*

Sharpe, Private Investigator for the Police Department of the City of Chicago, United States of America. This was stamped with an official-looking city seal. Written in pen were the words, *I hereby authorize my assistant Thomas Segovia to enter Blenheim Park and to cross police barricades at any place in the town of Woodstock.* It was signed by Mrs. Sharpe and dated.

Petra found the same thing, but with her name.

Both said *"What?"* simultaneously. Mrs. Sharpe was certainly full of surprises.

"Calder would faint!" Tommy said. "Assistant Investigator for the Chicago Police? I always knew she was a tricky one!"

"Will faint," Petra corrected as they hurried up the stairs to get their passports.

CHAPTER TWENTY-THREE

▲ ▲ ▲ Ten minutes after leaving Mrs. Sharpe, Tommy and Petra walked up to a police line at the Woodstock Gate to Blenheim. An officer looked at their cards, grunted, then said, "Oh, yes! The Boy's dad said the two of you would be here. Go along, then, looks like you've got your credentials! And no more trouble, d'you hear?"

The kids nodded, and walked through the massive stone entrance into the park.

Because of the high walls, neither had seen anything but photographs of the place. The real thing was a shock.

"It's GIANT!" Tommy gasped.

Petra turned her head in a slow circle. "It's art!" she whispered. "The way the palace fits with the bridge, and then the sweep of lawn and water — we're inside an old painting, Tommy!"

Tommy pulled on her sleeve. "Come on, they're staring at us. Police assistants don't go ga-ga about the scenery."

Petra glared down at his head, and nothing was said for a long time. They hurried along an endless road that led toward the maze, both feeling small in an extra-large landscape — small and not at all like a team.

It was Tommy who broke the silence. "Calder must have been lonely walking around here, especially after sunset."

Petra nodded.

Both were remembering that Calder always avoided the dark in Hyde Park. How could he possibly have chosen to hide here for a couple of nights? He wasn't the kind of kid who'd go off on his own for days and not think about his family, either. What could be so important that he'd stay out of contact for so long?

Tommy then said, "We'll reason like Calder. I know how to do that."

"Yup," Petra agreed stiffly. "So do I. We can try."

They walked in silence for the next ten minutes, both busy with troubled ideas.

Tommy was thinking to himself that even if there were treasure around and Calder were breaking the rules, he wouldn't be digging for it on his own. Not Calder, who was more interested in patterns and shapes than in keeping things. Except for his pentominoes, that is — he'd almost had a heart attack every time the Button made him leave them in his locker. So if it wasn't treasure, what could be keeping him away?

Petra was wondering, again, what game Calder could possibly be into — a game that involved a stolen Calder sculpture and the word *WISH*? Maybe he'd left another note for his dad, and the note got lost. Or maybe he *couldn't* leave another note.

"Tommy." Petra stopped walking.

Tommy stopped, too. "What?"

"What if Calder is stuck somewhere? Or trapped. Kidnapped. I had a dream —"

Tommy shook his head quickly. "Don't say it. Let's just concentrate on what we're doing."

"Okaa-y," Petra said slowly. "I guess you're right. It doesn't help."

Tommy sucked in his cheeks and shrugged, as if being right was nothing new. Petra rolled her eyes.

On their way to the maze, they passed oak trees that had to be hundreds of years old. Gnarled and bent, some had gaping hollows big enough to hide a couple of kids, hollows you could step into without ducking. They peered quickly into each one, and found strange knotholes and knobs but no sign of Calder. At last they arrived at the high brick walls surrounding the old kitchen garden; the hedge maze was not yet visible.

Tommy and Petra paused in front of the gate.

"We're here, Calder," Petra said softly.

Tommy startled her. "Hey!" he shouted. "Help us! We're trying hard to find you, and you've gotta give us some hints."

Petra made a sound that was half laugh and half shush, mostly because it didn't seem smart to be making so much noise. Tommy spun quickly in her direction and growled, "Think you're the only one with ideas?"

Suddenly she missed Calder more that ever, and her eyes burned. Tommy was always defensive, and always misunderstanding her. She stepped through the gate and sped up, passing a small, very old model of the town. She would have knelt down to peer in windows, but could feel tears prickling.

She ran the last twenty feet across a cropped lawn, hopped over a large puddle, and disappeared between the high walls of green.

Tommy watched Petra's back hurrying ahead of him, her chin down and her black ponytail bouncing. He missed his buddy Calder more than ever. Petra was so — what? Big? Not just that. *Irritating*, because she thought she knew what she was talking about. Calder never gave Tommy one of those looks. And he didn't talk about funny ideas like art, either. They just did things, and somehow understood each other.

Tommy kicked at a stone, chasing it toward the entrance to the maze. The stone bounced sideways across the gravel walk, and Tommy stopped short.

It had landed near a small disk that lay just off the path. Clots of mud and loose pebbles were scattered around it. Tommy picked it up. *What?* Had someone dropped this? No, it still had dirt clinging to it, as if it had been scuffed to the surface by a shoe.

The metal was old, very worn, and brown with flecks of green. There was a woman on one side, just barely visible, sitting on a large, round ball. She held a spear in one hand and a plant — or was it a small flag? — in the other, and her hair was pulled back in a tidy bun. Her face was rubbed clean, with just the tiniest suggestion of an eye. The letters *BRITANNIA* curled around the edge of the design, and Tommy saw tiny numbers on the bottom. Could that be 1752? What a find! An ancient coin!

On the other side was a man's head, a man with a grumpy face — you could see one scowly eye and a hook nose. *GEORGIUS II*, Tommy spelled out, and then *EX*. He spat on the coin,

and rubbed it carefully on his pants. No, it was *REX*. Tommy knew that meant king — King George II! What a discovery!

What mattered of course was finding Calder, but this was definitely awesome — 1752! Tommy thought back to Mrs. Sharpe's stories on the plane, stories about how long people had lived on this piece of land. There must be far older treasures all around. Maybe they were as common as bottle caps were at home. Maybe people picked them up all the time.

"Petra!" Tommy shouted. "PETRA! Where are you?"

No answer. A breeze ruffled the leafy walls of the maze. They'd seen no one else since they left the entrance to the park, not even any police. And this was a part of Blenheim that was made for families and children. It was kind of eerie.

"Petra!" Tommy shouted again. No reply. He slid the coin deep into his pocket and hurried toward the opening of the maze.

▲ ▲ ▲ Inside, Tommy rushed along, jumping over mushy spots. One turn, a branch in the path, now another — still no sign of Petra. He stopped. "Petra!" he bellowed again.

Silence.

He could hear someone moving slowly, slowly on the other side of the maze. Or was that the wind? The bushes forming the walls of the winding paths were so thick that in most places he could barely see light between the leaves. He thought of Calder by himself in this huge park, by himself at night. A nasty shudder rippled down Tommy's back, as if someone had touched him with an icy finger. He spun around — still no one in sight. Reaching into his pocket, he formed a fist around the coin. Help me, he said silently. Help me to find Calder.

REX, he thought suddenly. I have a king in my pocket! A king and a woman warrior of some kind. What if the people on the coin had wanted him to find them; what if they had extra powers. That was the kind of thing Petra would imagine, he realized, and shrugged. Maybe she wasn't all that bad. Being alone with her wasn't great, but being by himself was a lot worse.

He straightened his shoulders, glanced both ways, and walked ahead. What looked like a dead end became a curve. Following it, he came to another fork. Again he heard a tiny shushing sound, like someone running a hand along the bushes. Where was she? Well, two could play at this game.

He decided to tiptoe.

Step, step, step . . . Tommy kept glancing over his shoulder. The bushes were getting taller, and the sun had disappeared behind clouds. He felt as though he'd gone in at least ten different directions and hadn't gotten any closer to the center of the maze. Then he saw something black moving near the ground, in a path parallel to his. He froze. Boots? If so, they were big. Petra had sneakers on, and they weren't black.

He crept farther, looking for another low gap in the bushes. The hand gripping his coin was now sweaty, but he didn't dare let go. Who was this person in the maze with them? What if it was a man who already had Calder and had just grabbed Petra?

He could no longer see the dark shape moving. Had this person seen him, too, and was he now a target?

He rounded a corner and a line of black crows whooshed upward.

It was then that he saw Petra lying facedown across the middle of the path.

CHAPTER TWENTY-FOUR

᭦ ᭦ ᭦ The night that the five men picked up the *Minotaur*, all went smoothly, or so it seemed.

The transfer of the sculpture onto the market cart, the quick stenciling of the words WISH-WISH with yellow paint, the silent return of the cart on its rubber tires, pulled by the men in boots, black gloves, and black stocking masks: seamless. No lights went on in the town, no windows opened.

Just off the main road, outside the formal entrance to Blenheim, the sculpture was hurried down a dirt road into some woods. All went as planned, without even one passing car.

As far as the five men knew, there were no witnesses.

The sculpture was taken to a huge, deserted barn on an estate that had stood empty for over a year. The men waited there for the American who had hired them to turn up. The agreement had been that he would meet them at the barn that night, with a truck. They would move the sculpture from the market cart into the truck. Having found a way to enter the park along a remote farming road, he'd ride with the men, and then tell them exactly where to unload the piece of art. The payment was to be in cash, in five envelopes. The American had explained that he was acting on behalf of a larger interest.

The man never came.

The five men bolted the barn doors at dawn and agreed not to leave each other until they heard from the American. After all, what if he gave all five payments to one of them, and that one ran off with the money?

The men called home that morning and made their excuses, then stayed in the back of the barn, mostly napping and glaring at one another. By the second day, when the man who had hired them still hadn't turned up, they began to make plans.

They couldn't tell the police, could they? After all, they had stolen something worth millions, something that had been given to the town of Woodstock. But if the man had run off, wasn't the sculpture theirs to dispose of?

And then they heard a discussion on the radio of some scheme called the Calder Game. A part of an American art exhibit, it was inspired by the same artist who'd made their sculpture. The game involved everyday people balancing ideas, but in unexpected ways — it all sounded quite crazy. The suggestion was that a Calder sculpture and a Calder boy, both out of sight, might be a part of an elaborate game or a teasing message, especially with the yellow WISH-WISH left as a hint.

This was the excuse the five men needed. They had no intention of being a part of anyone's joke. Wishes, indeed! If the man who hired them could play, so could they: They'd sell the sculpture.

That afternoon, the men called a friend who handled large food deliveries, and borrowed a truck big enough for the *Minotaur* to disappear in. Their plan was to pack it in hay and head clear across Europe. Maybe they'd be able to unload it in Germany or Switzerland.

That night, a large Cadbury truck with a heavy load made its way south, headed for the English Channel. Five men were crowded into the front cab. A fine rain had begun to fall.

Wish, wish . . . The words swept back and forth with the windshield wipers, filled the truck, and rushed to fill the darkness ahead.

CHAPTER TWENTY-FIVE

▲ ▲ ▲ "Petra?" Tommy's voice had risen to a squeak.

Her head popped up, and she waved a small piece of yellow plastic. "Nope," she said, in such a matter-of-fact voice that Tommy suddenly felt enraged. "It's not a pentomino."

Who was *she* not to be frightened? And hadn't she heard him calling?

"I thought you were hurt!" Tommy shouted at her. "And I heard someone moving in the maze, someone else."

Petra sat up. "Really?" She looked both ways.

"Really!" Tommy said in his meanest voice. He decided not to mention the crows.

Still on the ground, Petra crossed her arms. "You know what? I think it's just you and me, Tommy, no one else, and if we keep getting mad at each other, we'll never find Calder."

Tommy was quiet, and Petra continued, "You're a good finder, we both know that, and

I'm — well, I'm not sure what, but I do have surprising thoughts when I'm writing, and sometimes things get clear to me." Petra was up now, and had stuffed what was left of her ponytail into the back of her sweatshirt, making a lopsided hump.

Tommy smiled, surprising even himself. At least you couldn't accuse Petra of being a fussy kind of girl.

"I'm sorry," he said suddenly. "I'm sorry I'm sometimes such a jerk."

Petra reached out and gave him a lightning-quick hug. Tommy's heart thudded violently and his cheeks turned brick-red. When his nose squashed against her sweatshirt, he caught a whiff of something clean and flowery — something like a folded sheet.

"Truce," Petra said.

"Truce," he agreed, digging his hands deep into his pockets. "Hey! I forgot to show you, I was so scared you were dead!" Tommy pulled out the coin.

"Whoa," Petra breathed. "Is this real?"

"I think so," Tommy said. "It's all beat-up, and look: Here's the date 1752 on one side. It was in a bunch of dirt just next to the path."

"Wow, 1752! I've never touched a coin this old before. I wonder where it's been all these years?" Petra's voice was dreamy, then suddenly business-like. "Hey! How about we get out of this maze, then head for the magical well, the one that was near the really old labyrinth. Rosamund's Well, remember? Then maybe old plus old, the coin near the well, you know! Maybe it'll add up to some luck."

Ordinarily, Tommy would have made a *this-is-silly* face, but something inside him was shifting. He almost believed that he and Petra could be buddies. "Fine, let's do it," was all he said.

Then he had a thought, a thought that seemed to come directly from Calder's brain.

"Here's something else about the coin: One plus seven plus five plus two equals fifteen. And then there are all the fives in Chicago at the MCA show. And Calder especially liked the size of ten-piece pentomino rectangles, remember? And wait —" Tommy counted on his fingers, his mouth moving. "'Alexander Calder' has fifteen letters!"

"Multiples of five! Cool, Tommy." Petra was beginning to think Tommy's black, cannonball head looked smart, and not just stubborn.

They hurried on through the maze.

"I know we passed this broken branch and that purple candy wrapper," Tommy said gloomily. "At least twice before."

"I know, I can't believe this is so hard," Petra said. "But at least we're together."

At least we're together. Tommy couldn't believe the words.

"You didn't seem too scared when I found you," he said.

"But I was," Petra said simply.

"Imagine how it would feel to know a minotaur was around the next corner," Tommy added.

"Or charging right behind you!" Petra shuddered.

"The idea of hide-and-seek in a maze is really

a nightmare, isn't it?" Tommy glanced behind them. "It's like someone is following you and you can't see them and you can't hide. Not in time."

"Right, you can't plan ahead because you don't know where you are. Or where the hunter is," Petra added. "I mean seeker."

"I wonder if Calder liked it once he got in here," Tommy went on. "You know how excited he was to be going into his first life-size maze. I wonder if he was scared, too."

"I'll bet he loved it," Petra said. "We're only afraid because we don't know where he is. Because being lost isn't a game anymore."

Tommy nodded. Neither said anything for the next two stretches of path, and then suddenly, on the next turn, they were at the end, and could see the lawn of the Kitchen Garden.

"At last!" Tommy leaped over a puddle. "I think I like paper mazes better," he added.

"Definitely," Petra agreed. "Ten times better!"

Once on the grass, they knelt down and unfolded their map.

"We're right here," Tommy said. "Got a pen?"

Petra pulled one out of her jeans pocket. "And a small notebook, if you need it."

He shook his head, and made a mark on the path where he'd found the coin. "There, X."

"How about an X where the WISH-WISH stencil is, in the town square?"

"Done." Tommy scrawled another X.

"The Xs can mark places we know are important, but that we don't yet understand," Petra said.

Tommy nodded.

Perhaps, Petra thought to herself, the crossed Is that formed the X were a symbol of her and Tommy, of them combining forces to find Calder.

"Symbols," she said aloud, suddenly embarrassed.

"Symbols," Tommy repeated, and Petra wondered if he'd had the same thought.

▲ ▲ ▲ As they approached Blenheim Palace, the police were everywhere. The building was very grand and formal, and Tommy and Petra agreed that Calder would never have gone inside, at least on his first day in the park. After the maze, he would have been busy exploring the gardens and maybe the Rosamund's Well area.

They wandered behind the house and smelled hot chocolate. A sandwich wagon had been set up for the detectives and officers.

"Should we?" Petra asked. "I'm starving."

"We've gotta eat. This is safer than leaving the park and then hoping they'll let us back in, don't you think?" Tommy said. Petra still wasn't used to him sounding so relaxed and unprickly with her.

"Yup." She nodded happily, then mashed her hair into a fresh ponytail and brushed the dirt from the maze off the front of her sweatshirt.

They marched up to the wagon, trying to look as if they ordered police food every day.

"I know, I know, you're the Chicago kids," the officer behind the lunch counter said, and made his eyes big and then squinty. "We heard about you on the walkie-talkies."

Petra elbowed Tommy not to say anything, and he didn't. They studied the selection of sandwiches. "We'll have a cheese-and-pickle and a chicken-and-tomato. And two hot chocolates," she said, trying to sound like a busy person who ordered lunch all the time.

The detective wouldn't take money ("No, no, this is all paid for!"), so they thanked him politely and hurried off into one of the gardens.

"Ha, you sounded just like Mrs. Sharpe!" Tommy crowed.

"I tried," Petra said, not insulted at all. "Here, how about this wall?"

Neither realized, until they were eating, that they were facing a large and very bare bottom, a woman's bottom attached to a statue in the fountain. There were plenty of bare, female bottoms in the Art Institute, in Chicago, but not too many out in the parks. Petra looked around. Here, bottoms were everywhere. There were even quite a few bare, male bottoms. Both Tommy and Petra pretended, as they ate, that they hadn't noticed all the nakedness.

After lunch, they walked toward the Queen Pool, as that part of the lake was called. If they crossed the Vanbrugh Bridge, the old one with arches, they should be able to find the well.

Heading off into a clump of trees, relieved to be leaving the police and the nude bodies behind, they talked as if their talking was nothing astounding. So much had shifted since breakfast.

"Maybe Calder went through the maze, and then . . ." Tommy's voice trailed off. "Strange that no one remembers seeing him in the park with another person."

"I know, my mind just keeps hitting dead ends, too." Petra sighed. "It's hard not to imagine bad things."

"But doesn't this place seem pretty safe to you? I mean, all the English stuff seems so — *polite*. Like everyone has good manners."

Petra laughed, remembering the bottoms. "I think people here just sound polite because we're not used to their accents and some of their vocabulary. But I know what you mean, and I guess it *is* safer, statistically, than Chicago."

Just as she spoke, a man's deep voice boomed nearby, and another shouted back. They heard the sounds of running feet and a boat engine. They broke into a trot, reached the top of a hill, and slithered down the bank to the crowd of police officers gathered near a small, blue police boat.

From where they stood on a pile of rocks, both could see: Curled in the stern of the boat, wrapped in red blankets, was a body.

CHAPTER TWENTY-SIX

▲ ▲ ▲ As Tommy and Petra learned that day in Blenheim, passing time isn't a steady thing. People try to measure it, but some days seem to have years packed into them, and others pass in the blink of an eye. Some days matter, and others don't.

That day in England was an endless one, a day filled with extraordinary glimpses and brightly colored shocks. It was a day neither kid ever forgot.

It had started with Mrs. Sharpe treating them like adults, then there was Tommy's coin, then they miraculously started to like and help each other. Now this: the body.

Side by side on the bank of the Queen Pool, both felt as though they were falling out of their world and out of familiar time. No, falling wasn't a fast enough word. They were hurtling.

Calder . . . Calder dead . . . Calder under blankets . . . Calder.

By the time they heard the word *man* coming from the police, both were weeping. Seeing the two of them frozen in place, faces crumpled, one of the officers walked over.

"Now, now, no one's dead," he said consolingly. "At least not yet. No, it's not your mate. It's a man."

Petra sat down on a too-hard rock. *Man,* she thought, they found a *man*. Tommy busily blew his nose into a bush. *Man,* he thought, *man,* the word was a miracle. Both wiped their faces on sleeves and a number of other surfaces. Petra's ponytail snagged on a branch, the elastic snapped, and she practically disappeared in a puff of black curls. The officer only shook his head.

"Off you go, you two. We've a lot to do. Man's in need of emergency treatment before we can get him back to town. Head injury, and not a pretty thing." The officer's voice went up and down in a matter-of-fact way, as if he were talking about groceries or an approaching rain shower.

Petra and Tommy climbed the bank, silent

and suddenly exhausted, and headed on shaky legs in the direction of the palace. Crossing the bridge to Rosamund's Well was clearly not possible until the police had finished in the area. Neither kid had to speak to share; good and bad were so tangled that words wouldn't help, at least not yet.

She looked down at her shoes and Tommy's shoes, walking, walking, walking, one step at a time . . . walking while some man lay injured in the boat.

"Calder walking, I can't wait to see Calder walking," she said aloud.

Tommy nodded. "I know," he said. "Calder walking."

▲ ▲ ▲ As they approached the palace, they saw Walter Pillay and Mrs. Sharpe in the distance. Mrs. Sharpe held onto Walter Pillay's arm, which was bent at the elbow. They were headed for the Garden of the Bottoms.

Petra and Tommy ran to catch up. They shared the news.

"Really!" Mrs. Sharpe said. She stood up straighter.

"My god," Calder's dad said in a weak voice. "Who was he? Was he conscious?"

"Don't know," Petra said. "We were just so relieved — I mean . . ."

"Yes," Calder's dad said quickly. "Of course."

"Come, let's sit down and talk," Mrs. Sharpe said. "There are seats in the Temple of Diana, and I've brought a couple of fresh Rock Buns. I know, dreadful name." The old woman waved her walking stick in the direction of a small stone building, and off they went, the other three feeling relieved, at that moment, to be ordered around.

Open on one side, the building looked like a tiny Greek temple. The four sat in a row inside, on a stone bench.

Mrs. Sharpe spoke first. "This is where Winston Churchill asked his wife, Clementine, to marry him," she said. "She remarked later that she was expecting he would, and while she waited, she watched a beetle crawling on the

floor. She thought that if the beetle crossed a certain crack, he'd ask, and if it didn't, he wouldn't. It did."

Mrs. Sharpe's businesslike voice was comforting. She pulled out a package wrapped in brown paper, and everyone shared the buttery scones.

"Tommy and I were on our way to the bridge when we saw the body in the boat," Petra said. "I mean the *man*."

"We've been trying to do exactly what we thought Calder would do here," Tommy added. "We started at the maze."

"Reasonable," Mrs. Sharpe said, surprising them all. She hardly ever sounded this uncritical.

"How did you get those Chicago Police cards for us?" Petra asked, thinking it might be a good moment. "Were you really a private investigator?"

"I've always investigated, and I've always been private," Mrs. Sharpe snapped, her tone making it clear that the subject was closed.

Petra nodded and swallowed.

Walter Pillay, who had been quiet, cleared his throat. "Well, I've done some research."

There was a silence. The other three waited.

"I started by finding out that Alexander Calder's *Minotaur* was privately owned before it was given to Woodstock and then installed in the square three weeks ago. Although the donor wanted to remain anonymous, I did some back-door digging, and managed to find out who had it for the past ten years: It was a man by the name of Arthur Wish."

Tommy and Petra both said, "WISH-WISH!" in the same breath, and then elbowed each other. Mrs. Sharpe said nothing, but one eyebrow rose slowly.

"And guess what," Walter Pillay went on. "He lives in Chicago. Or lived: No one seems to know where he is. He hasn't appeared in public for at least a couple of years, and people in his founda-tion explained that he travels, communicates by computer, and is rarely available."

"Foundation?" This was Mrs. Sharpe.

"Oh, yes. He's a millionaire, perhaps even a billionaire, and collects modern art. He owns many, many Calder sculptures and mobiles; I believe he has one of the largest private collections in the United States.

"He started a foundation called Free Art: Share It! five years ago. The idea was to make art available to everyone — he donated the funds that made it possible to offer the Calder show at the MCA without charging admission. And he gave a great deal of money that went into organizing the show, and even setting up the Take Five room. He believes that the art world is stuffy, and that too much of it is about having money and making money, not celebrating the experience of art. As he put it, he wanted to help give art back to the people, especially to children. He's put lots into community programs that invite kids to experience and make art in their own ways. And believe it or not, that's his real name: Arthur — or Art — Wish."

"Art Wish!" Petra said, delighted.

"Wonderful name," Mrs. Sharpe said slowly. Tommy nodded.

Walter Pillay went on, "I heard from Isabel Hussey this morning that your teacher Ms. Button has been back to the Calder show many times, on her own. She apparently noticed a drawing for an anonymous mobile that consists of a plan to place five Alexander Calder sculptures in five different public spaces around the world. One would be in England, and the other four in Japan, Chile, Turkey, and Russia."

"Whoa!" Petra said. "What an idea!"

"The Button? Back at the museum? What's gotten into her?" Tommy asked, his face a study in both alarm and surprise.

Mrs. Sharpe waved at them to be quiet.

Walter Pillay continued, "The entire mobile would be visible and complete once the five sculptures were donated and installed. There's a sketch of one of the sculptures on the sheet of paper, and guess what? It's a drawing of the *Minotaur*, with the words 'Market Square, Woodstock, England.'"

Mrs. Sharpe thumped her cane twice on the stone floor of the temple, but didn't interrupt him. Petra's and Tommy's mouths were open.

He went on, "I also found out that Art Wish loved to visit England and admired some of their forward-thinking ideas about art. For instance, museums in England charge no admission fee these days, making art far more available.

"Then I found, from reading interviews online, that there is one modern artist in particular that Art Wish admired. His name is Banksy, and he's British.

"People either love him or hate him. He's an expert troublemaker, and the strange thing is that he could be anyone. He doesn't, you see, have a face."

CHAPTER TWENTY-SEVEN

⋀ ⋀ ⋀ Noticing Tommy's and Petra's horrified expressions, Walter Pillay added quickly, "Nobody knows what he looks like. He's somehow managed to protect his identity."

"Ohh," Tommy said, looking relieved. "So he could be pretending to be someone else. He could be anyone."

"Exactly, and he could be anywhere," Walter Pillay said.

"He could be the man in the boat," Petra murmured.

"Exactly," Walter Pillay said again. "Banksy started out as a graffiti artist, and of course that's illegal. It's considered vandalism in most countries, at least by law. But he's talented and witty and has some powerful ideas about giving art back to the people, about defying mindless authority. He also has a wicked sense of humor. He creates things, sometimes crazy, funny things, to make people stop and think and question. In 2005, he made four small pieces of art, and over a number of days smuggled them into four major museums in New York City. He stuck them all up on the wall without getting caught. Then he managed to have photographs taken — he must have been working with a friend or assistant — and recorded how long it was before his 'fakes' were spotted and taken down.

"Each of his pieces of art made fun of the traditions of a particular museum, but in a subtle way: For the Metropolitan Museum, there was an old-fashioned portrait of a lovely woman with a gas mask on her face, and for the Museum of Modern Art, a plain image of a British soup can. The Brooklyn Museum was given a painting of a colonial American soldier holding a spray-paint can, with anti-war graffiti visible behind him. At the Museum of Natural History, Banksy hung a real beetle equipped with fighter wings and missiles, elegantly displayed in a glass case. The one at the Metropolitan was only up for two hours, but the others were up for six days, eight days, and an amazing *twelve*! Maybe that says something about how carefully most people look at what they see in museums.

"Banksy's comment was that he hated the way museum art was selected by a rich few, people with money who decided what made a piece of art worth looking at or owning. He thought art should also be by the people, for the people, and free.

"No one seems to know if Banksy and Art Wish have ever met, but Art Wish clearly loved what Banksy was saying, and wanted to join in, in his own way. His intent was to give away some of the museum art he owned, and give it away so that it was accessible to the public. And he apparently wanted the local people to decide if a sculpture belonged in a certain place. He wasn't going to force his ideas on anyone.

"And the people in Woodstock..." Walter Pillay paused, and seemed to be choosing his words. "It's very sad, really. As far as I can see, they didn't want the sculpture. Except, perhaps, for one girl."

Calder's dad scratched his head. "Calder and I saw her taking pictures of the *Minotaur* late one afternoon. And then we saw her get in trouble with her father, even though she pretended just to be drawing the sculpture when he showed up. Somehow, she seemed intensely interested in it, and he didn't want her to be.

"The afternoon that I saw Calder in the square talking with a man, I was about to get off the bus and I happened to see this same girl taking another picture of the *Minotaur*, but out of a second-story window. Her photograph must have included Calder and the man, and I thought she might have caught the man's face. Since no one's been able to identify him, it could be important — very important.

"And then I saw her duck out of the bed-and-breakfast this morning. I'm afraid I frightened her by leaping out the front door and shouting." Walter Pillay paused, and shook his head. "Strangest thing, but she turns out to be a cousin of Miss Knowsley's. I can't get her to talk, or to give me her name. And Miss Knowsley just looked flustered when I asked. She didn't answer, either.

"The girl seemed nervous and worried when I asked about the photo, and wouldn't look me in the face. She whispered something like, 'No film in the camera. I was just practicing.'

"Then I asked her if she knew the man in the square, and she shook her head violently and ran off." Calder's dad shrugged and held his hands palm up. "I suppose the next step is to point her out to the police, but I'd hate to get her in trouble with her dad, who seemed like quite a brute. I'll bet he didn't know she had the camera. Funny little thing, she only seems to wear black."

Everyone stayed silent, thinking about this latest piece of news. Petra was frowning, thinking back to the girl in black who seemed to be eavesdropping when she and Tommy were in the town square talking yesterday. Could it be the same girl? She hadn't seemed quite as innocent to Petra.

Walter Pillay sighed. "So, back to what I *did* manage to find out: Arthur Wish has a tragic past. He married early and had two children. His entire family was killed years ago in a terrible car accident. He never married again, and apparently has been somewhat reclusive right up to the point at which he became unavailable. It does seem, though, that he's still alive. Otherwise, who could have given the *Minotaur* to Woodstock? Unfortunately, I can't seem to get any deeper into his personal history than that. Like Banksy, he's learned to protect his privacy."

"So who stenciled WISH-WISH on the market square the night the *Minotaur* was stolen?" Tommy asked.

"The Thames Valley Police suspect Banksy, although I imagine that's all wrong. Stealing a huge piece of art isn't something he'd do, as far as I can tell."

"But why would a real criminal bother with painting the WISH-WISH?" Mrs. Sharpe mused. "Doesn't seem likely."

"You mean it might have been done by someone local, someone who didn't like the sculpture."

"Possible, although no one in Woodstock was supposed to know the donor's name. And if it was someone local, why would they want to deface their precious town square with graffiti? It doesn't make sense." Mrs. Sharpe was fiddling with her gold bracelet, sliding it off and on her wrist.

"Well, here's what I think," Walter Pillay said. "The sculpture disappearing must be some kind of game. Art Wish was playing the Calder Game when he shared his marvelous plan to give away five Calders, but he must have been a philanthropist who had many enemies. Someone bold always does. Perhaps the wrong person in Chicago, someone besides Ms. Button, saw the Calder Game mobile that Mr. Wish made and decided to jump in for personal reasons. Maybe they came to Woodstock and are here now. Maybe they're playing their own Calder Game."

"Hey, maybe Art Wish had some secrets that weren't so nice," Tommy said. "Something he did a long time ago. Sometimes that happens, an old crime catches up with a person."

Mrs. Sharpe gave Tommy a piercing look. "Very astute, boy. Close to my own thoughts."

Tommy sucked in his cheeks and looked at the ground.

"So . . . if *my* Calder got roped into some kind of game, and it felt important enough, that could explain his being gone. And if it was a game, he'll be fine — even if it was some game that was meant to make fun of Art Wish. I can't imagine anyone would want to organize anything seriously bad here, can you?"

The question hung in the air as a police car drove slowly toward the temple and stopped in front. The officer driving rolled down his window. "Got news, Mr. Pillay. Not about your son, I'm afraid," he added quickly, seeing Walter Pillay's eager expression.

The policeman cleared his throat. "It's the man in the boat. He was found in a grove of bamboo — I've always said we should trim that stuff — halfway between the Cascade and the bridge. Hidden. We've identified him. A businessman by the name of Arthur Wish, an American. We hope he'll live. Ever heard the name before?"

CHAPTER TWENTY-EIGHT

▲ ▲ ▲ The news about the man by the lake spread like wildfire in Woodstock. Miss Knowsley, who had been shopping at the butcher's, dropped her bag of partridge breasts with a *whump* into the sawdust underfoot. She clapped both hands over her mouth and wailed, "My Artie! Oh, my poor laddie!" She had to be helped outside and then back to her house on Alehouse Lane. The police who now filled the town had heard her words, and two detectives escorted her back to her house.

She sat in her front room and wept for a good half hour, every few minutes muttering things like "Should have known!" or "Should never!" over and over. The detectives waited patiently.

When both detectives had offered their pocket handkerchiefs and she had used most parts of both, she settled down and told this story:

Her nephew, Arthur Wish, had grown up in America. Miss Knowsley's sister, Rosamund, had gone to school in Chicago, at an arts college, and there met a man and married him. He made lots of money, but apparently it wasn't a happy marriage, and he never allowed his wife to return to England. ("Knew she wouldn't come back from there!" Miss Knowsley sobbed. "A prisoner, just like the other Rosamund!" More sobs, and then, "A prisoner in that nasty place, an endless maze of city streets shaped in a grid. Oh, I've seen pictures!")

At age ten, Arthur Wish was allowed to come to Woodstock for a summer, on his own, and stay with his aunt. Miss Knowsley rocked back and forth in her chair and moaned, "Fishing in the Queen Pool, oh, he loved that! And the woods, and all the places to play, the Grand Cascade and all. . . . It was a paradise to him, poor little fellow, being brought up in that dirty city."

"He — he —" A fresh round of tears started, and the detectives waited patiently. "He wanted to give something back to England, you know? He never forgot about Woodstock." More tears.

"He came to see me, and told me about the *Minotaur*. I'm afraid I didn't like it." Here there were more tears, and Miss Knowsley had to wipe her glasses on her skirt. "I told him so. I don't approve of modern art, and I told him it didn't belong!" Miss Knowsley broke off and rocked back and forth miserably.

"But I never told my neighbors here who he was, I swear it! He said he wanted the gift to be anonymous, and I never told!" Miss Knowsley rocked some more.

"I don't know if he realized, being from a big American city and all, how close a community like this can be. How close . . ." Here Miss Knowsley wept so loudly that one of the detectives got up and patted her on the shoulder.

His cell phone bleeped just then, and the detective excused himself and answered it in the kitchen. When he returned, his face was troubled.

"I regret telling you this, ma'am, but it looks like Arthur Wish was injured by a blow to the head, a nasty blow that came from behind. It doesn't look like an accident. In addition, it seems he was dragged into the bamboo and left there. This is now an assault-and-battery investigation, possibly with intent to kill. We'll need to ask you a few questions."

CHAPTER TWENTY-NINE

▲ ▲ ▲ After delivering the news about Arthur Wish, the police drove Walter Pillay and Mrs. Sharpe back to Woodstock. Mrs. Sharpe needed a nap, and Walter Pillay went directly to the hospital. If the injured American regained consciousness, Calder's dad wanted to be there to ask him if he'd met or seen Calder.

There was a spooky, hide-and-seek symmetry to the appearance of the collector who had anonymously given *Minotaur,* a man who admired the secretive Banksy, and the disappearance of the two Calders.

Walter Pillay wondered if he could identify Art Wish. Was this the man Calder had shaken hands with in the town square? If so, there wasn't a moment to lose.

▲ ▲ ▲ Petra and Tommy headed off in the direction of the Cascade, which they were sure Calder would have wanted to explore.

It was a long walk. They passed a giant grove of rhododendron bushes, one with dark rooms lurking behind shiny leaves. Looking for Calder, the kids ducked inside: only spiders. Out again, they passed a round rose garden encircled by a lacy trellis, and a bunch of exotic fruit and evergreen trees. They were then able to touch the largest tree either of them had ever seen, one with a sign that read, CEDAR OF LEBANON. It was as wide as a road, and seemed to reach upward forever.

The path marched on through a field filled with amazingly unworried pheasants, and soon they heard running water. As they hurried down a steep hill and around a corner, the sound of the Cascade grew louder and louder.

The River Glyme pounded cheerfully over a rough tumble of boulders; the falls raced downhill for a stretch of twenty to thirty feet. At the base, a narrow footbridge was being repaired. Boards were missing from the center, and the bridge was blocked with a DO NOT CROSS sign.

Petra and Tommy walked as close to the rocks as they dared, and then stood side by side, thinking.

"The bridge looks fine. What do you think? Should we?" Tommy said.

Petra shrugged. "What would Calder do?"

Tommy grinned. "He probably already did."

Petra nodded.

They started across, balancing only on the metal supports along the edges, in the same way they'd walked in the hall outside their rooms the day before.

"Hey! You there!" a voice shouted. "Back to the bank!"

A police officer charged down the path behind them. Tommy and Petra froze, and the bridge beneath them slowly began to move. It buckled, it swayed, the kids yelled, and suddenly everything around them was dark and green — dark and green and very cold.

When Petra went in, her glasses came off. By the time she bobbed to the surface, looking for Tommy, everything around her was a blur. The

officer had waded in up to his chest, grabbed both of them firmly, and was dragging them out of the water as if they were two bad babies. All three slipped and fell on the moss and algae by the bank.

"Hey!" Tommy said. "Let go!"

"My glasses, I know where they came off!" Petra said, her teeth beginning to chatter. "Right there, the minute I hit the water. Let me go back for them, I've got to have them, I can't see a thing! I don't have another pair with me! Please!"

"We'll have to send a diver back for them, I'm afraid," the police officer said firmly. "Right, we're calling for a boat. Got to get you two back, no waiting around. You'll catch your death of cold, you will!" The officer made a call on his walkie-talkie, then marched them up the bank to the top of the falls and pushed them down on a rock to wait.

"But what if her glasses drift downstream?" Tommy asked. "I could jump back in and take a quick look. It isn't deep, you know."

"And have you drift downstream? Not on your life!" the officer said.

Petra and Tommy huddled together, shoulder to shoulder, instinctively trying to stay warm. Petra took a last, blurry look at the top of the Cascade, and suddenly thought she saw a flash of color by the top of the falls.

"Tommy! I could swear there's something yellow over there near the big rock. Bright yellow. See it?"

Just as Tommy turned to look, the police motorboat roared into the shallow water nearby, stirring up mud from the bottom and clouding the water. The moment was over; Tommy and Petra had to climb in. They were wrapped in heavy blankets, the officer who rescued them poured water out of his boots and accepted some brandy, and the boat sped off, headed back toward the town.

▲ ▲ ▲ Woodstock was packed with curious faces, now that an ambulance had gone by. Some looked worried, some sad, some pleased. When the police car pulled up at the guesthouse and Petra and Tommy climbed out, there was lots of tsk-tsking and oh-mys. Petra, without her glasses on, couldn't be sure if a dark blur on a bicycle was the eavesdropper — but the thin, black shape did pause at the back of a group of people as the kids squelched toward their door, and seemed to be staring at the two of them. When Petra squinted hard in that direction, *pffft!* the figure was off, blond hair fluttering, with a quickness that reminded Petra of the way the girl had spun around yesterday in the square.

Mrs. Sharpe didn't respond to a knock on her door, and no one answered Miss Knowsley's phone. Petra and Tommy took hot showers, changed, and met half an hour later in the hallway outside their rooms.

Tommy stared at Petra. "You look different," he said.

"I know, my hair's wet so I wrapped it up with this stupid scarf." Petra looked embarrassed. "To keep it from getting too crazy."

Tommy shrugged. "You look kind of like that picture. You know, the one with the girl looking over her shoulder. The one on Ms. Hussey's wall at school."

"The Vermeer?" Petra's eyebrows shot up happily, and she turned away to hide her face. "Okay," she went on quickly, "let's find someone to bother about my glasses, and maybe that will get us back in the park. Hey, did you put your passport out to dry on the heater?"

They talked all the way down the stairs and out into the street. Tommy complimented her on trying to dive back into the Glyme to get her glasses, and she thanked him for offering to do the same. Together, they were different people than they had been the day before; together, they had become parts of something larger than themselves, something that was slowly becoming visible.

CHAPTER THIRTY

▲ ▲ ▲ The number at the Temple of Diana that afternoon hadn't really been four; it had been five. After Walter Pillay, Mrs. Sharpe, Petra, and Tommy left that afternoon, an ovoid creature, black against the yellows and reds of fall, hustled over to where the group had been sitting. He licked up several chunks of scone, as well as a number of ants who had arrived first.

Pummy now sat on a rock at the edge of the Cascades, looking intently into a shallow pool. Miss Knowsley, who had been busy with her own worries that day, had forgotten to feed him.

Pat, pat — one paw went in and out of the running water, in and out. *Pat, pat* — he pulled the paw back, shook it, and licked it vigorously.

He tried again. Whatever Pummy was watching moved gently in the current. The yellow floated to one side, caught in a pile of red leaves, then drifted back down against the black rock, feathering back and forth like a small fish. The

water above the yellow sparkled, catching first blue and then flashes of bright white.

Pummy watched. "*Yeow,*" he said, and blinked his eye slowly, thoughtfully.

He looked up, hearing the rumble of a car approaching through the park. He licked his paw again and turned back to the pool.

"*Yeow,*" he said to the three men in black approaching the bank.

"You're a big thing," one man said. He marched past Pummy and down the hill, got his mask and tank in place, and waded in to the Glyme at the foot of the Cascade. The other two policemen watched from the edge.

Pummy went back to fishing in his pool. *Pat, pat . . . pat, pat . . .*

Below the broken footbridge, the diver swam back and forth for several minutes. Then he popped upright and waved Petra's glasses in the air. The roar of the Cascade drowned out voices, but the divers standing on the bank waved back.

As the three drove by in the police van, Pummy sat quietly, his yellow eye following until they vanished into the woods.

▲ ▲ ▲ Miss Knowsley was rocking. Back and forth, back and forth — rocking as her mother had before her, and her mother's mother. She closed her eyes and rested her head against the back of the chair.

She'd been angry. But what had she said?

Her nephew had promised to give a delightful piece of art to the town. She had pictured a nice little nymph, or something like the sculptures in the gardens at Blenheim. But when she'd seen the *Minotaur* . . .

She'd told Artie it wasn't appropriate, it was an outrage. When he'd argued back, insisting that Woodstock would grow to love it, that the British had a marvelous sense of humor and that a naked garden sculpture was much more inappropriate than this, she'd told him that he didn't understand.

"You're not from Woodstock. You don't recognize the importance of tradition," she had
snapped. Then, meanly, she'd said, "Americans
make a mess of everything. They think having
money means they can behave in any way they
like, and that the things they prefer can and
should be forced on everyone else. Well, they're
wrong, dead wrong!"

Artie had looked so hurt. She had seen the
flatness in his eyes. "So you're against it," he
had said. "Maybe with time —"

"Never." She had cut him off, and then had
left the room. She hadn't even said good-bye; he
had let himself out. That was just over two
weeks ago, and the last time he'd set foot in the
house on Alehouse Lane. Tears ran down Miss
Knowsley's cheeks as she remembered it.

But what exactly had she said in the village
that day? What had she said, that day she was so
angry?

Everyone talked . . . talked over tea in the
shops, or while buying onions or posting a letter.
Everyone talked in Woodstock, and nothing went

unnoticed. And a little town like Woodstock was used to taking care of things in its own way.

Chilled, Miss Knowsley thought back to a man from the United States who had moved into the area ten years ago and talked loudly about how to improve this and that — water pressure, food deliveries, even church services. He'd disappeared, hadn't he? There had been Missing Person signs up for days, then someone had scrawled *GOOD RIDDANCE*, in black, over the pictures. The man had never been found.

Artie! She should have defended him. But he didn't understand, did he? Well, he'd been warned.

He was, in truth, an American. And did Americans understand a warning? They sometimes didn't know when to stop.

And then the news she'd just gotten from the girl, a distant cousin whose father had called to say he wouldn't be home for several days, maybe longer. Family was family, but Posy Knowsley knew that the girl's father, Nashton Rip, was no saint, even though he *was* a relative. Nashy had

241

been saying things around town ever since the *Minotaur* appeared in the square. Now he was mysteriously gone, along with the sculpture and boy. Something made her not want to tell Walter Pillay that the girl would be staying at the bed-and-breakfast until her dad returned. Oh, dear, another thing to hide!

Oh, the dreadfulness of it all! How had everything gone so wrong?

Miss Knowsley squeezed her eyes tight as the tears dripped off her chin.

CHAPTER THIRTY-ONE

▲ ▲ ▲ "You two are to stay out of Blenheim Park from now on. No special permissions." The officer who reached out of the van to hand Petra her glasses jerked his head in the direction of the park.

"Nothing but trouble in there," he added.

"Thanks for returning these to me," Petra said, and looked at the ground. Tommy kicked at a pebble.

"That's right, mates, solid ground is where you belong. No more of this detective nonsense. We'll find the boy, don't you worry, and meanwhile the two of you run off. That's it, no reason to stand around the entrance here."

"And how is Mr. Wish?" Petra asked politely.

"In hospital. Coma," the policeman said.

Petra and Tommy were silent. Art Wish . . . unable to speak, unable to tell or explain.

The van drove on, and the police at the gates turned their backs on Tommy and Petra.

Tommy pulled the map out of his pocket. The two studied it, whispered for several minutes, then headed off down a side street that ran parallel to the park wall.

▲ ▲ ▲ "We'll flip the coin," Tommy suggested. "If it's the lady, you go over. If it's King George, it's me."

"And whoever goes in first gets that delivery door in the wall open. There's probably a single bolt on the inside."

"Right. Simple. You ready?" Tommy pulled the 1752 coin out of his pocket, spat on it, then rubbed it vigorously on his pants.

Petra's mouth twisted into an *eeuw* shape, but she stayed quiet.

"Gotta get all the dirt off it before flipping," Tommy said. "Okay." He blew on the coin once, then cupped it in his hands.

"Superstitious?" Petra asked. Tommy shrugged. "How about I flip it?" she added.

Tommy, to her surprise, handed it over.

The coin felt warm. "I'll let it fall on the ground," she said.

"Afraid you can't catch it?" Tommy grinned.

Petra shrugged, then tossed the coin into the air. She stepped back, and it bounced once on the dirt and rolled. It landed with the woman up.

"Guess that's me," Petra murmured.

"Let's do it," was all Tommy said. He popped the coin back into his pocket.

Eyes peering out of a nearby window saw the boy brace himself against the wall, facing the layers of stone. He stood between two parked motorbikes. The girl looked both ways, then climbed up on the seat of one of the bikes, which wobbled. The eyes watching blinked once, then again.

From there, she placed one knee on the boy's shoulders, then the other. Slowly, holding on to the wall, she stood, one foot on each shoulder.

The boy looked up, and the girl hissed, "Don't!"

"Hurry, you're heavy!" the boy whispered.

The girl placed both hands on the mossy top

of the wall and slowly inched one leg up and over. Then she stopped. "Uh-oh, I'm stuck!" she whispered down.

The boy placed both hands on her ankle and gave a mighty heave upward.

There was an "*OOF!*" and then a *whump,* and then silence. The boy anxiously looked both ways. "You okay?" he whispered.

He stood quietly in front of the wall, listening. A minute went by. The door didn't open. "You okay?" he repeated, louder this time.

The eyes watching from behind a lace curtain blinked again.

The boy waited. He called again. Still no answer. Soon a police car approached, driving slowly toward the boy. It stopped. The boy talked to the driver for several minutes, then climbed into the backseat.

As the car pulled away, a rolled piece of paper flew over the top of the wall.

CHAPTER THIRTY-TWO

⋀ ⋀ ⋀ Stunned, Petra lay on her side. She struggled for air. Knocked the wind out of myself, she thought. Just a fall. Better in a moment. Suddenly, with a gasp, she was breathing again. The air was delicious.

She'd landed on a brick walk, under a huge tree. No house was visible. The path was overgrown, and dense bushes on either side met in an unfriendly mesh in the middle. Like interlocking fingers, Petra thought with a shudder. Hundreds of reaching fingers.

She rolled the other way and looked up at the door. A smear of old cement covered the lock and what looked like the slot for a bolt. The door was locked, and locked for good.

"Tommy!" she called, as loudly as she dared. Silence, just the whispery sound of a breeze in the bushes . . .

No! She wouldn't get frightened. Why hadn't she and Tommy made a plan in case only one of them got over the wall?

It felt all wrong to be in the park without him.

She thought suddenly about Arthur Wish, and how he had ended up with a head injury, lying in the bottom of a boat. Think like Calder, she told herself firmly. Calder and Tommy. She and Tommy had made a decision, and she knew Tommy would find her.

Just in case, she felt in her pants pocket for her pen and notebook and sat up, her back to the wall. She scribbled a quick mobile-note, tore it out of her notebook, rolled the page into a tube, and tied it firmly with three long grass stems. There. She tossed it over the wall.

▲ ▲ ▲ As Petra hurried through the bushes and trees in Blenheim Park, the light began to fade and the colors around her shifted. The lake turned black, and Blenheim Palace glowed yellow in the low sun. I won't look at the woods, she thought to herself. Anyone could be in those woods. She shivered, scuffing ahead through red leaves that were everywhere — glorious bursts of color that now reminded her only of fresh blood. Murderers must love the fall; so easy to hide the evidence. But what am I thinking! She shook her head as a line of geese flapped west, tracing a shaky path between stone, water, and sky.

▲ ▲ ▲ Tommy was driven back to the guesthouse by the police. They had asked where "the girl" was, and he had lied, saying she'd gone back ahead of him.

He hopped out of the side of the car, gave the officer a friendly wave, and stepped into the doorway. As soon as the car turned a corner, he popped back out on the street.

Fingering his coin, he wandered through the bendy roads and paths that connected the buildings in the town. Very little was set up as a grid; the old part felt more like a maze. Had someone planned it that way? All of the streets radiated from the central square, which had once had its own minotaur, but now held only WISHes.

Tommy knew Petra would have liked his thought, and hey — it would work for a poem-mobile, too:

NO-MINOTAUR-ONLY-WISHES-HERE

Those five words could float around one another and make you think of all kinds of unexpected things. The *wishes* and the *no* balanced, and the *minotaur* and the *here* were both kind of surprising — but the *minotaur* and the *wishes* were also good together. He was getting used to the Calder Game. Thinking in fives wasn't so hard, and it had cool results. He understood why Petra liked this game.

Tommy realized, to his surprise, that he already missed her. This had certainly been one weird day.

He spotted interesting things on his walk, but nothing helpful — a tin pail, a chair with a broken leg, a long piece of red yarn that wound around several corners. And then he saw it: a sturdy, long bench that might have come from a church. It had a broken board in the seat. Perfect. Once it got dark, he could use it as a kind of ramp or ladder against the park wall. He shoved the bench deeper into the weeds by the side of the lane and tossed a bundle of newspapers in front of it. There, it was hardly visible now.

He wandered away from the bench, whistling, and headed back to the guesthouse. Upstairs, he knocked on Mrs. Sharpe's door.

"Come in." Her voice was crackly.

Tommy opened the door. "Mrs. Sharpe?"

"Who else would it be? Anything to report?" she asked, then blew her nose.

"Well, no, not really, but yes, Petra and me — well, we went back out after falling in the river and now we're both tired. Petra's taking a nap, and I need one, too," Tommy blurted in a rush. "We don't want dinner."

Mrs. Sharpe took off her reading glasses and studied the boy. "Yes, I heard about that little accident. And am I supposed to believe you?" she asked. She blew her nose again. "*Rrrump-a-ra-RA!* I've got a cold. I always do when I travel," she growled.

"Yes, I mean, believe me. And sorry about your cold," Tommy said. Both hands were deep in his front pockets, and he squeezed the blue button in one and the coin in the other. The coin stuck to his palm. He tried to scrape it off.

Mrs. Sharpe eyed the restless pocket. "Didn't hear any creaking in the hall when the girl went into her room to nap just now, and walking through this building is like making popcorn. Noisy."

Tommy was ready for this one. "You told us to think without rules, remember? So we've learned to walk silently down this hall. You know, one foot on each side."

Mrs. Sharpe sniffed and leaned her head against the back of her chair, closing her eyes. "Sleep well, boy. Be sure to be at breakfast in the morning, both of you, eight on the dot."

As Tommy backed out, he could have sworn he saw Mrs. Sharpe peeking at him with one eye.

▲ ▲ ▲ After sharing his suspicions with the police, Walter Pillay had been allowed to see Art Wish that afternoon. The man remained unconscious. Was this pale person with the bandaged head the same man he'd seen in the town square with his son? It was hard to say. After all, he'd only seen him from behind. Calder's dad remembered a black jacket slung casually over the man's shoulder, and the officer on duty confirmed that Art Wish had indeed been wearing a black leather jacket when he was found. But weren't there thousands of black jackets in England?

Walter Pillay wished, with every ounce of his being, that he had looked through that bus window with greater care. As he left the hospital, he was assured that he'd be called immediately if Mr. Wish regained consciousness. He strode toward Blenheim Park, walking rapidly and almost at random, looking for any possible trace of his son. He found only Pummy.

By then it was late afternoon, and the black cat sat calmly on a rock by the Cascade.

"Home, Pummy, home!" Walter Pillay said, remembering Miss Knowsley's words. The cat glared at him and meowed once. His loud *"yeow"* sounded just like an angry *"ne-a-o-o-o!"*

Slowly, daintily, Pummy lifted one paw, tapped the surface of the water, and then shook it. Had he said no, and then waved at something in the pool?

Walter Pillay shook his head and muttered, "Home, Calder, home," but his second "home" wobbled into a sob. It had been a long and horrible day, and they were approaching the fourth night that his son had been gone.

Four nights! It was unimaginable that something had happened to Calder, and Walter Pillay, discouraged as he was, refused to think it.

Sighing, he turned around. On the walk back, he touched every leaf within reach, as if touching their aliveness would help to protect his son.

He needed to call Yvette, who had been sleeping earlier. She was still in the hospital, in Chicago, and he was already thinking of how best to tell her that the police hadn't found a thing today, only a man in a coma — an American with an ugly head injury. Plus, this now-silent man was the person who had owned the stolen sculpture. It was not good news.

And what had he discovered today? An over-fed cat with one yellow eye. Glancing back at the falls, Walter Pillay frowned. Not many cats fished in the evening.

He shook his head. Everything felt odd and everything felt wrong, as if he were suddenly inside a world in which cats talked back and a cozy English village could swallow a boy.

CHAPTER THIRTY-THREE

▲ ▲ ▲ Calder had been here, just four afternoons ago. And he absolutely, positively went to the maze.

Petra stood at the edge of the stubbly field dotted with ancient trees. She and Tommy had decided that afternoon that returning to the maze area was the best idea. After all, that's where the symbols were, and symbols were something Calder understood. The codes he'd always invented so easily were made of symbols, and maybe he saw the maze as another code. If its shape held something that could be decoded, Tommy and Petra needed to take another look, a closer look. There was still light. In the distance, Petra saw the high brick walls of the Kitchen Garden.

When she and Tommy had walked toward the maze that morning, she'd noticed the trees but hadn't been frightened by them. Now, as she approached alone, they looked strangely alive. Twisted figures gesturing with claw-like arms:

257

guardians, or perhaps running people frozen by an angry force into trees, the stuff of myths and fairy tales. The oaks seemed to be signaling, saying, "Look! See! I'm not a tree!" She pushed the thought away. Childish, she said to herself fiercely.

She placed a hand on one of the trunks and patted it, as if to show she was friendly. The tree was at least six feet thick, and the inside hollow. The dark entrance looked horribly like the mouth on a giant face, and she now saw a long, broken nose and two mean, misshapen eyes.

Petra was just thinking she would *never* crawl inside, not for anything, when she heard a man's cough, and then a low murmur. Voices, but coming from where? She spun around, checking the shadows on all sides. Two figures, but not men in police uniform, walked quickly through the gates of the Kitchen Garden, headed her way. Their faces were hidden, their hands tucked into jacket pockets.

There was no choice. In a flash, she ducked inside the tree. At that moment, she would have

given a great deal to be somewhere near Tommy's cannonball head.

▲ ▲ ▲ Sneaking out of his room as soon as it was dark, Tommy hurried back to the alley where he'd left the bench. There weren't many streetlights in Woodstock, and the high stone walls created deep channels of black that snaked away from the town square in all directions. Tommy shuddered and dove in.

Moving the bench was more difficult than he'd thought it might be. It was long and heavy. He walked a short distance down the alley and spotted a wheelbarrow in someone's front garden. If he could just borrow that . . .

Heart pounding, he stepped into the garden, grabbed the wheelbarrow by both handles, and began to trundle it out. Every step or two it squeaked loudly.

Tommy froze, took two steps, froze again. He looked back at the house. The front rooms were dark. Lucky — the family was probably in the kitchen cooking or eating.

Holding his breath now, he squeaked back down the alley to where the bench lay. Then he dragged it across the top of the wheelbarrow, balancing it with one knee. The wood rubbed angrily on the metal, and he knew he was making a dreadful amount of noise. He'd *never* make it through town and back to the wall!

Unless . . . earlier that day, while waiting for Petra to open the door, he'd noticed a back entrance to one of the graveyards. It opened onto a winding brick path that traveled the length of the graveyard and out onto High Street, in the middle of town. He could use that, but going in the opposite direction.

Hey, he told himself fiercely, *a graveyard is a graveyard*. Just a bunch of old stones! Stones and bones. He was almost there.

Squeak, squeak, squeak. He trundled the wheelbarrow to the end of the alley and stopped, catching his breath. He'd rest and count to ten, and then, when the street was empty, dash across with his load.

One, two, three, four, five — a car zoomed

around the corner, heading directly toward him. He froze, turning away from the headlights. The car sped past.

The street was now quiet. An occasional leaf rustled under the crime tape that still surrounded the WISH-WISH; a dog barked in the distance. A door opened, and then closed again with a thud. He thought of Calder, all alone somewhere. And Petra, alone in Blenheim Park. He suddenly felt braver; they were all in tough situations. There was nothing to do but keep going.

Gripping the wheelbarrow handles, he wove across High Street, pausing every few steps to nudge the bench with his knee. It was almost a relief to reach the dark entrance to the grave-yard. Almost.

CHAPTER THIRTY-FOUR

⋀ ⋀ ⋀ As the men approached Petra's tree, one switched on a flashlight, and the beam bounced around the field. It had gotten dark much sooner than Petra had thought it would, and at the moment that was a good thing. She held her breath, pulled back against the inside of the trunk, and tried not to think about what might crawl into her hair or down her back.

A wind had come up in the last few minutes, a sudden breeze, and it swished across the tops of trees, blurring the voices. Petra strained to hear.

"From the boy," one man said.

"You think?" said the other. "Never found," and then, "dead by now."

The words bumped and jostled in an ugly, sharp-cornered way. *Dead by now, dead by now.* They might be talking about Arthur Wish — it couldn't be Calder. No, she had never imagined, for more than a moment, that Calder was dead. She knew Tommy didn't believe it, either. Tommy! Could it be Tommy they were talking about? If someone could hit a full-grown man on the head, they could certainly get rid of a troublesome boy. Panic rippled down the length of her spine, and she realized that no one, no one in the world, knew exactly where any of the three friends were at that moment. *Dead by now, all three gone* — the words flashed through her mind.

The men passed her tree and headed toward the lake. She peered out.

The wind had picked up, gusting now. It blew directly in her face, as if to push her back toward Blenheim Palace and the lights of town. She stood next to the tree, breathed deeply, and told herself to run as quickly as possible toward the high brick wall.

What was a little dark, anyway? Just no sun, she reminded herself as her sneakers pounded toward the opening. Just dark, all three fine, she whispered to herself again and again, spinning the words outward into a mobile in her mind. They floated into *dark-three, all-just-fine* and then into *all-fine, dark-just-three*. She went back to repeating *just-dark, all-three-fine* until the syllables turned into *one-two, three-four-five*.

They would find him tonight, she and Tommy would rescue Calder, she could feel it in her bones. She stepped into the shadows of the old garden, and something stiff and cold whipped into her face. She shrieked and stumbled.

▲ ▲ ▲ With a heavy load and no flashlight, the graveyard walk was a nightmare. Under his breath, Tommy whispered every bad word he knew while he bump-bumped along; the bad words made him feel braver. He'd never realized how impossible an old brick path could be. The front tire of the wheelbarrow got stuck every few feet, falling into holes left by missing or broken bricks. The path was slippery with moss, and corners and edges that had once been flat now reared up in a dangerous, invisible landscape.

The bench collided with a gravestone and tumbled off the wheelbarrow. With an especially fierce curse, Tommy looked around. Long, spooky shadows reached from the corners of the graveyard, and the pale markers glowed eerily in the blackness. Nothing was straight, and that made it all the more frightening; stones were tilted or sunk, trees twisty, the path a mere memory of right angles. Nothing in England is new, Tommy found himself thinking, and suddenly felt homesick for a world that wasn't nearly as old or mysterious, a world where people didn't walk into a park and vanish, or come out almost dead.

A car drove by on High Street, in front of the church, and the headlights dragged a crooked wedge of shadow across the graveyard, a dark triangle that became the top of a tombstone rising, rising as if being pushed from below. Tommy knew that was nonsense, but his heart jumped, and in a split second his wall of words shattered into terror. He imagined bony fingers, spirits angry at being disturbed, graves opening up to swallow him. *New, sorry I wished for new*, he thought quickly, hoping any nearby ghosts would forgive him. *Old, old, only old*. With a surge of energy, he dragged the bench back on top of the wheelbarrow and set off in a staggery run for the back gate.

Eyes followed his back as he hustled, as fast as possible, between the graves.

CHAPTER THIRTY-FIVE

▲ ▲ ▲ Just as Tommy scrambled over the wall into Blenheim Park, a large Cadbury delivery truck pulled up behind a greenhouse not far from the main gate. The five men in the truck were exhausted and hungry. Hours of worried argument had led them to abandon their plans to sell the huge Calder sculpture; no one wanted to end up in jail. The *Minotaur* lay buried, packed in hay, in the back of the truck.

One by one, the men climbed down from the front seat. The first walked toward Woodstock, and the second away; the third set off across a field, the fourth scaled the wall by the park, and the fifth hitched a ride from a passing car.

All felt cheated by the American who had hired them. All resented being a part of what they suspected was someone else's elaborate game.

▲ ▲ ▲ A couple of hours later, a local farmer opened up the back of the truck marked *Cadbury: You dream it, we make it.* It was parked on his neighbor's property, and his neighbor wasn't home.

Inside, the farmer found bales and bales of hay. A brisk wind banged the doors of the truck back against the sides, and wisps of hay flew outward into the surrounding hedges and fields.

Aside from the hay, the truck was empty. He shrugged; probably a joke of some kind. He'd call the police in the morning.

CHAPTER THIRTY-SIX

▲ ▲ ▲ "Fall."

It was only a word, but everyone in the room clapped.

"Artie, dear! It's your Auntie Po! Fall! Yes, you had a little fall, my darling!"

Arthur Wish only shook his head. "Fall," he said again. "Under."

"Yes, you fell down!" Miss Knowsley crowed soothingly. "You can tell us everything later, just rest for now."

A police officer standing in the back of the room stepped forward and touched Miss Knowsley on the shoulder. "With all due respect, ma'am, the boy. We need to ask him about the boy."

"Oh, yes, the boy," Miss Knowsley fluttered, getting up from her chair. The officer sat down and leaned toward the man in the bed.

"Ever seen a boy by the name of Calder Pillay? Can you tell us where he is?" the officer asked loudly.

Art Wish opened one eye. Everyone held their breath. The lid slid closed, as if without the eyeball's consent. "Fall," he said again, both eyes shut.

"Falls." The word was barely a whisper.

Miss Knowsley heard the final 's' and looked sharply at him. "Was that fall*sss*, Artie?"

"Maybe it was 'false,' ma'am," the police officer ventured.

"Oh, don't confuse things!" Miss Knowsley said irritably. "I know my Artie!"

A purring snore came from the bed; Arthur Wish was fast asleep.

▲ ▲ ▲ After her visit to the hospital, Posy Knowsley began to think. What had Art been trying to tell them?

Fall, and then fall*s* . . . Of course, he might have been trying to tell them that he'd fallen, but why struggle to say that? And why the 's'? Falls . . . there was only one set of falls near Woodstock, and that was the Grand Cascade.

When she got back to her kitchen, Miss

Knowsley made herself a cup of tea. She *tsk-tsked* to herself about the fact that Pummy was still out, and then she began to think, stirring her sugar around and around, faster and faster, until the tea was stone cold.

She remembered something she hadn't thought about in decades.

When Art had visited Woodstock as a boy, he'd spent hours in Blenheim Park. After the sad horrors of growing up in a large American city — she couldn't even imagine, not even for a second — she understood that the freedom was delicious.

He'd loved the fishing, and loved playing on the rocks at the end of the lake. One day, after weeks of going to the Cascade on his own, an older man, a Woodstock local, had beckoned to him. Art had hurried over.

"Secrets around here, my boy," the fisherman had said. "Secrets of a fabulous nature." Art had later repeated those very words to his aunt.

And then the man had gone on to tell Art that one of the dukes of Marlborough, over two centuries earlier, had had a magical platform constructed in the falls. An ambitious engineering feat, this room-like ledge had eventually collapsed back into the tumble of rocks. The question was, had it disappeared entirely or was there still, somewhere in the falls, a hidden space?

Miss Knowsley now wondered whether Art had told the boy the story of the secret platform. They could have gone to the falls and . . . what? If the boy had fallen down some crack, he should have been able to get out. The Glyme wasn't terribly deep or wide there, and the current was slow. What could possibly have happened to him? And why else would Art be saying it? Did Art know some *other* secret about Blenheim that he'd never told his aunt?

Miss Knowsley's thoughts swirled around and around with her teaspoon.

A pity she couldn't talk with neighbors at this hour. But then again, she'd already done a bit too much of that. No, the person to speak with would be returning to the house, and soon.

When Walter Pillay opened the front door that night, Miss Knowsley was waiting for him. Her cheeks were pink, and she was rubbing her hands, rubbing them so quickly that they looked like a flurry of knuckles and veins.

"Quick, we need to go!" she said.

▲ ▲ ▲ As Tommy dropped over the top of the wall into pitch blackness, it occurred to him that he might be falling into a deep hole, or worse — onto rock. If he was hurt, no one knew where he was. Not one soul. Well, he thought grimly as he crashed into a bush, that makes three of us. Three kids, lost in an ancient hunting ground. He stood up, rubbing a sore knee. At least he'd escaped from the graveyard. But did mazes have ghosts? Tommy shook his head, trying not to let his imagination go wild. *Wild*. Tonight the word sounded very real, almost like a wail.

His coin! He reached into his pocket, and there it was — small, round, reassuringly warm. He squeezed it tight in his palm, thinking suddenly about Calder and his pentominoes. His coin was for luck. Were Calder's pentominoes, also? He was growing more like both Calder and Petra with every passing hour: first noticing a meaning behind the numbers on his coin, then spotting the multiples of five, and now hearing the word *wild* as if with new ears.

Petra would understand how the coin worked, and that it held powers. Tommy decided he'd never sell it for money if he kept it, not now. Petra would respect that decision. It could be his talisman. Tommy remembered Ms. Hussey talking about a classroom lucky stone, a round stone with two rings that crossed. That made him think of the crossed Is in WISH-WISH. He squeezed his coin, and wished with all his might.

He was standing in a deep pocket of woods, and the wind had risen overhead. Branches whipped and cracked, and Tommy didn't think he'd ever heard anything so lonely.

Walk away from the wall, he found himself thinking. Walk away. The woods will end, and you'll be able to see where you are. There was no reason to pull out the map in his back pocket. He wouldn't be able to see a thing. He'd find his way to the maze, no problem. Petra must be so frightened, by herself in the park all this time. Why hadn't they planned for something going wrong before she went over? It was the first stupid thing they'd done together, and for some reason that cheered him up.

He began to walk, moving between huge trees. He'd count each step. One hand stayed deep in his pocket, clutching his coin.

Eight, nine, ten — *whang!* A branch he stepped on snapped up and knocked him off his feet. He was on the ground. His pants were snagged, and one leg pinned beneath him. Something had bitten his elbow. Could he have stumbled into an old animal trap? Cautiously, he wiggled his arms and legs.

At that moment, he heard heavy footsteps crunching over branches and brush, the steps of a large man. Tommy froze, his eyes huge.

Crunch, crunch. The steps came closer. He lay absolutely still, listening to raspy breathing.

Whoever belonged to the steps was listening, too. *Crunch, crunch* . . . then a sharp snap and a low growl.

Was this *human*? Tommy's mind was racing. Were there *bears* in this part of England? Or a lunatic who had been shut up in the palace for years and just came out at night? Tommy closed his eyes as tightly as he could, as if to make himself vanish. He squeezed his coin. I wish, he thought to himself. I wish.

Crunch, crunch, crunch . . . The steps were headed away. Tommy lay still as long as he dared. He listened to the branches sighing overhead and the distant squeaking of something that sounded like a huge wheelbarrow. What if he'd broken some centuries-old rule by trundling through the graveyard at night, and an angry ghost now was pushing his wheelbarrow into the park, looking for him? Anything seemed possible.

Other things were moving around in the park that night, no question about that. Other things besides two kids from Chicago.

Tommy got slowly to his knees.

▲ ▲ ▲Petra had fallen over a low fence and was lying on her face inside the Kitchen Garden. She opened one eye.

No one in sight. She'd tripped. Was someone behind her? Should she move?

Then she realized she was looking into a tiny window, on a tiny house. Next to it was a small stone church. Had she become a giant, like the storybook Alice? Suddenly, the thought felt funny, and funny felt safe. She lifted her head, looking to see what had hit her in the face.

Ivy! Just a runaway clump of ivy, hanging down from the wall. Relief flooded in, and she sat up.

She was next to the model town she'd seen earlier today, when she and Tommy had been fighting. She half expected to see tiny people walking between the houses — nothing felt impossible now. But there was only the sighing of the wind outside the walls of the garden, the wind mixed with deep drifts of shadow, and the high, pitch-black bushes of the maze. A giant, empty world towering over a small, deserted one.

279

Where should she wait? She knew Tommy was coming; she just hoped he'd be fast, *very* fast. And then she heard a voice humming, and a man's cough, and the *squeak-squeak* sound of a bicycle. Or was it two?

The sounds came closer. Could it be the police? On bicycles, and at night? If so, should she give herself up?

The squeaking stopped, and Petra heard a dull thud, a grunt, and another thud, as if two people were fighting. Then she heard someone breathe, "Idiot!" as if both surprised and angry.

Later, Petra didn't remember thinking at all. Her feet carried her lightly, as quick as the night wind, across the garden.

She slipped into the dark entrance to the maze.

CHAPTER THIRTY-SEVEN

▲ ▲ ▲ Two of the five men who had stolen the Calder sculpture were old friends, and both knew that the caper had only just begun.

When they'd abandoned the truck on the outskirts of Woodstock, everyone had agreed that it had been a crazy dream, to think they could sell that monstrous thing and get away with it.

The two friends had managed a few seconds alone together, at the back of the truck. In that time, one mouthed the word *reward* to the other, and both jerked their heads toward Blenheim Park. There was sure to be a tasty thank-you offered by the police for the return of this sculpture.

Half an hour after the five had split up and walked in different directions, the two men were back outside the truck, carefully loading the *Minotaur* onto a hay wagon.

The sculpture was very heavy, but the two were masons and knew how to handle weight. They managed to tip and roll and tug until the sculpture was balanced on top of the old boards. Next they tied a large plastic covering over the top, one that said THAMES VALLEY POLICE — DO NOT DISTURB. The letters crumpled as the men lashed their load down with strips of police tape, wrapping it around and around with quick, expert strokes.

"That's it. That'll slow the questions, anyway!" the smaller man panted.

The larger man nodded and spat. "More useful here than in covering that infernal graffiti and roping off the square! The stupidity of the police! As if graffiti could tell them anything! Wishes, my foot!"

"Wind's come up," the first man said.

"Move along then, not a moment to spare, let's head for the Hensington Gate." The big man rubbed his hands together, as if looking forward to a sporting event. "Here's how it'll go: We'll pull off on the side and toss a fistful of pebbles at the guard on duty. He'll look around with his torch, we'll give him a treacly knock on the noggin, and in we go. Nothing serious!"

The other man chuckled, then added, "Mere bagging expedition, that's all! Nothing to it!"

The two set off, pulling the wagon as if they were oxen, the largest man in front. It rolled slowly along the main road, dragging a sinister, lumpy shadow over the old walls of the park.

"Be able to get Georgie off to a proper school," the big one grunted. The load was so heavy that, as he pulled, his neck vanished between his shoulders, making him look more like a beast than a man.

"No counting eggs yet," the other cautioned.

"Who's counting eggs?"

"You!"

The men stopped, gasping for breath, and shared a swig of whiskey. They pulled the wagon into the bushes by the main gate to Blenheim, and all went so smoothly that it felt like a miracle: no passing traffic, no bicycles coming home late from the pub, no dogs.

The guard was a police officer stationed inside a police car, and he was fast asleep.

"His lucky break," the big man growled.

Without another word, they trundled at top speed around the police car and into the park. The officer slept on. Pulling as hard as possible, the two hustled their weird-looking load down the long, straight road to the palace and up onto the old stone bridge that spanned the end of the River Glyme.

The plan was this: If police appeared suddenly, they'd throw up their hands and explain that they were just trying to get the sculpture to a safe spot, that they'd discovered it on the hay wagon. They might still be able to collect a reward.

And if they could do it, if they weren't interrupted, they would unload the sculpture on the top of the bridge, in all its glory, and then roll the wagon down the bank and into the lake, where it would vanish without a ripple. They'd then stuff the police tarpaulin and tape under a bush, sit down by the sculpture, and wait for morning.

The story was that they'd just entered the park to fish — something people in the town often did without permission, and no one really minded — and found the *Minotaur*. They didn't feel they could leave it, didn't have a cell phone, and were guarding this great piece of art until the police arrived.

After all, they were good citizens, everyone knew that, and had ancestors who had served many a king. In doing their duty by Woodstock — and wasn't that what they were doing? — they might soon be heroes, perhaps even rich ones.

CHAPTER THIRTY-EIGHT

▲ ▲ ▲ Tommy heard the splash. It was the sound of a meteor falling out of the sky, a huge slap of a splash. Now there was shouting in the distance. He began to run between trees, already frightened that someone could have thrown Petra off the bridge. Or was it Calder? Petra could swim, but Calder wasn't famous for liking it; he was too skinny and always shivered.

As Tommy ran, he realized that no, this was not the small splash of a person, or even two people. But a car? Maybe a police car had gone in.

He burst out of the woods on to the edge of a field. In the distance, maybe a quarter-mile away, was the famous Vanbrugh Bridge, the big one that led to Rosamund's Well. Police cars approached from either side, and dark figures seemed to be running toward the bridge from the direction of town. Flashlights bobbed. Headlights shone.

There was no sign that anything gigantic had just fallen, no sign except a curling arc of water, a wave that was rolling toward the Cascade and the River Glyme.

▲ ▲ ▲ Pummy, at the sound of the splash, had dashed under cover in the woods. He peered out as the wave rolled over the rock he'd been sitting on. The water swirled through pools and around boulders, cresting into foam and bubbles as it reached the edge of the falls.

After the wave had passed, something small and smooth gleamed on top of Pummy's rock. It was a piece of broken plastic, a piece about the size of a cracker. Even by starlight, it was easy to see the color.

Yellow. The piece of plastic was yellow.

▲ ▲ ▲ Petra, inside the maze and behind the high brick walls of the Kitchen Garden, heard nothing. She promised herself, as she crept toward the turn ahead, that she would memorize her path. She'd remember, and then she could escape quickly.

She stopped and listened; whoever had been

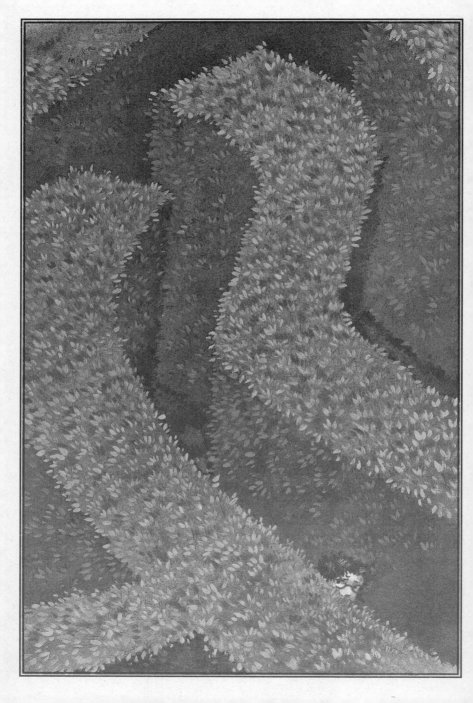

outside the walls was either gone, or . . . or . . . the thought was too scary. Why would any adult run silently across the grass and then enter this maze in the middle of the night?

Only a crazy person would do such a thing. *A crazy person.* Who had hit Arthur Wish on the head? And who had made Calder disappear? The dark thoughts rose in Petra's mind like a line of bubbles in a fish tank, bubbles that were hard to stop.

As Petra walked slowly, thinking *right-left-two rights-now left,* she told herself firmly to focus, not to think about anything but the next step.

Each . . . next . . . step.

Step.

Step.

She tried to force her mind back into the dark channels of space, pretending she was walking through a pentomino maze that Calder had designed. After all, wasn't a maze supposed to be about finding as well as losing? Wasn't it supposed to be fair?

She turned a corner, starting bravely down a path she couldn't yet see. Hadn't she read somewhere that a maze symbolizes what life is about? It's a journey filled with choice and surprise, lefts and rights, and finally an unseen end. She was inside a symbol made of symbols, what an idea! Petra shivered. Calder would enjoy the clean way one concept fit inside the other, but then he'd never been in this maze at night and alone.

Or had he? And what was *that*?

Petra heard something moving ever so softly and slowly, something walking on a path that ran parallel to the one she was on. No, she told herself firmly. The wind was still rising, and it was only air pouring through one of these green channels, a stiff breeze ruffling the bushes. And then she heard the snapping of a twig, followed by another.

She froze, her heart pounding. Should she go back? Forward? Suddenly, the lefts and the rights jumbled and spilled, rolling this way and that in her mind. *Left-right-right-left* — the words had become nonsense, like signposts in a nightmare.

Why had she run into the maze? Now she was trapped. *Trapped.*

Fighting panic, Petra held on to her friends. Tommy was also in the park alone, and he wouldn't panic. At least, he'd pretend not to. And what would Calder be thinking? He'd be puzzling and rearranging in order to calm himself. *Trapped, trapped* . . . Suddenly, Petra saw the letters of her name hidden in the word. Horrible! No, she thought, *trapped* is no place to find your name, and being inside a maze made of symbols doesn't help, not even one bit.

This was real, not a game, and it felt ugly: Whoever was in the maze with her could catch her, and no one would even see them struggling. She didn't stand a chance.

Petra's legs crumpled, and she sank down in the middle of the path. Where was Tommy? Maybe he'd never even found her note. She half rolled, half crawled under a nearby bush, squashing herself beneath the lowest branches. She pressed her head as close to the trunk as she could. *Wish . . . wish . . . if only.*

Two of the three kids were curled into a crescent at that moment, and two — but not the same two — were wishing, as if Art Wish's name and the yellow WISH-WISH stencil had opened up a new set of rules.

CHAPTER THIRTY-NINE

▲ ▲ ▲ That same evening, Mrs. Sharpe made a discovery.

She had visited the Woodstock library and taken out a number of books about the geography and history of Blenheim Park. In every spare moment over the last day and a half, she'd been reading and thinking and sifting ideas.

She knew the boy Calder liked mysteries and had a good mind for patterns and puzzles. He also understood numbers, and, she felt quite sure, understood them better than most people.

Mysteries. She was looking for mysteries at Blenheim. She didn't know how or why the Calder sculpture had vanished, but she wasn't convinced that the boy knew anything about that. Perhaps he had become curious about something else, and had gotten too close. He might have been poking around someplace he didn't belong.

But how did the collector, Arthur Wish, fit in? She thought of the Minotaur, of Henry and Rosamund, and of the two mazes at Blenheim, one legendary and the other very real. Games and myths . . . of course these were ancient myths, really just stories about bravery and revenge and love and loss, the same things that have always brought joy and pain. Could a myth come to life if connected with just the right game? But heavens! It was a silly thought, perhaps the thought of an old woman who had read too much about symbols. She refused to imagine that the boy had been consumed alive.

And then she read again, that evening, about the old viewing platform at the Grand Cascade.

Struggling to her feet, she went out into the hall and knocked at the children's doors. She should have known: Both were gone.

Mrs. Sharpe then put on her most sensible shoes and all of her warm clothing, and set off for the park. There wasn't a moment to spare.

She *stump-stumped* over the cobblestones, her shadow slipping lightly across walls and past quiet curtains. Once or twice she stopped to listen, and even to look behind herself.

What was that? She'd heard something — a rustling of fallen leaves — and hoped that as she walked, she walked alone. She knew about small towns, and knew that very little went unnoticed. She also knew that odd things could happen to anyone who disturbed the peace.

CHAPTER FORTY

⋀ ⋀ ⋀ Miss Knowsley, who had asked Walter Pillay to call her Posy, was standing at the Triumphal Arch, the town entrance to Blenheim, holding firmly to his arm. While hurrying through the dark streets of the town just moments earlier, the two of them had agreed on what to say to the police. It was just as they turned the last corner that they heard a tremendous splash.

In all the shouting and confusion, the officers at the gate didn't notice two figures ducking inside the high walls.

Minutes after the figures hurried off unseen, an old lady with a cane worked her way slowly toward the same entrance to the park.

⋀ ⋀ ⋀ By the time Posy Knowsley and Walter Pillay reached the bridge, there were at least five police cars. No one could figure out what or who had fallen into the lake, but everyone was examining the empty market cart. Ribbons of police tape waved mournfully from the edges of the cart, as if the party were over and the prizes gone — but what party? And which prizes?

Just as the detectives absorbed what Ms. Knowsley and the boy's father were telling them, that there might well be a secret room in the Grand Cascade that the boy had fallen into, Mrs. Sharpe arrived in the back of a police car, having commandeered it at the gate. Oddly, the old American woman backed up their theory. Then she added the sobering piece of news that the other two kids were missing, and had left no note about where they might be.

"But it's obvious," the old woman added briskly. "Where else *would* they be?"

Police walkie-talkies crackled, and an order was given. Calder's dad and Miss Knowsley were invited into the car with Mrs. Sharpe. Soon the police cruiser was bouncing along the road to the Grand Cascade, clunking over rocks and careening around ruts. With each jolt, Mrs. Sharpe poked the back of the front seat with her cane. Not knowing his elderly passenger, the officer driving assumed these jabs were involuntary.

As the four adults climbed out of the car at the top of the falls, a round, dark shape came hurtling out of the shadows. "*Yee-owww!*"

"Pummy, darling! Where have you been, you naughty boy?"

The black ball of fur could then be seen attacking a cracker that came out of Miss Knowsley's apron pocket. Unafraid of all the commotion, he blinked his one eye thoughtfully and looked around. He licked his whiskers, then licked one paw.

The cracker gone, he moved slowly and daintily, rock by rock, toward a boulder that was several feet from shore. Head on one side, he sniffed the small piece of plastic sitting on the top of his rock.

Tap-tap! He pushed the object with his paw, moving it gently. *Tap-tap!*

"Never seen a cat that fished like that at night," one of the officers remarked. "Saw him

earlier today, trying to get something out of that pool. Looks like he finally made his catch."

It was then that the group heard feet pounding along the path through the woods. It was the quick *bam-bam-bam* of a small person running. Everyone turned as Tommy burst out into the headlights, gasping for breath.

"Petra — in the maze — something moving in the woods, something big —" he panted, and Mrs. Sharpe surprised everyone, including herself, by giving him a hug. Tommy surprised himself all over again by hugging her back.

Then, before anything more could be said, Walter Pillay gave him a quick, *glad-you're-safe* squeeze that lifted Tommy off his feet. It was then that the boy saw Pummy on the rock, and an oddly familiar object next to Pummy's paw.

"Wait!" Tommy said as soon as he was standing again. "What's that?"

A flashlight beam whirled across the top of the falls, and Pummy's one eye flashed. "It's a pentomino!" Tommy shouted. "It's one of Calder's pentominoes!"

Walter Pillay was already splashing crazily toward Pummy, who hissed in alarm.

Next came a flurry of cat fur, slippery rocks, a father who went underwater, and a small wet head swimming furiously for shore. Everyone was shouting.

"Stand back!"

"Oh, Pummy darling!"

"The man's lost his mind!"

"He's got it — the first piece of evidence!"

Calder's dad stood, half sobbing and half grinning, the shiny yellow piece of plastic held high in the air. Everyone looked away as he kissed it, then waded slowly toward the shore, his head down.

It wasn't clear at all that the broken pentomino was a good sign.

CHAPTER FORTY-ONE

▲ ▲ ▲ A new quiet settled on the group as Walter Pillay and Tommy examined the shard together, busily theorizing about the pentomino being a signal or perhaps a message of some kind left by Calder. It wasn't logical, but neither is the need for hope. No one mentioned the fact that Calder never lost his pentominoes or left them behind — unless forced to.

A police officer reported the find through her walkie-talkie, but she shut the car door before speaking and didn't talk long. She popped back out of the patrol car, looking uncomfortable.

Mrs. Sharpe, watching in silence, now cleared her throat. "While the moving equipment gets here, perhaps we could investigate the maze. You heard what the young man said."

"I'll bet Petra's waiting," Tommy said eagerly. "Oh, yes, please! She's probably frightened out of her gourd. I know I was, while I was in the woods. We were planning to head for the maze once we got over the wall, but . . . it wasn't so easy."

It was now the officer's turn to clear her throat, but instead of lecturing Tommy, she asked, "Anyone like to go along? Might be a good idea to have a familiar face."

Tommy now looked agonized, glancing from the policewoman to Walter Pillay. Mrs. Sharpe said quickly, "I'll go."

The officer ducked back into the car to make a call for another vehicle and officer, one to drive to the Kitchen Garden with the old lady. She was in the car for quite some time, the walkie-talkie crackling. Those standing outside in the dark could see her rubbing her forehead. When she put the receiver down and stepped back out, her face was an odd combination of goods and bads. "News!" she blurted.

Several things had happened: In the last half hour, two local men had been arrested in the bushes by Rosamund's Well. They had been responsible, they said, for moving the *Minotaur* to the top of the bridge, where they claimed it had tipped off the wagon in a tremendous gust of wind and fallen into the lake. The men said that an American man had hired the two of them and several other local men — no names were given — to move the sculpture three days before, but then never turned up, as promised, to pay them. He hadn't given them his name. They insisted that they were just returning the sculpture to the police, but couldn't explain why they had agreed to steal the sculpture in the first place, or why they had then dragged the wagon into the park instead of simply placing a call.

"Claimed they had no cell phone, and didn't want to leave the sculpture someplace where it might be stolen," the police officer said, then rolled her eyes. "Again!"

Tommy glanced at Miss Knowsley. Her mouth had tightened into a shaky pucker. She looked like she was going to cry.

The officer hurried on to tell the group that a heavy construction vehicle was on its way, and that the rocks at the edge of the falls were going to be moved that night. They wouldn't even wait for dawn, now that a pentomino piece had been found. And Arthur Wish, in the hospital, had managed to say a little more. Here the police-woman paused.

"What?" Walter Pillay almost shouted.

"He has only said, 'Falls, boy in falls.' He said it twice." The officer looked sorry not to have better news on Calder. Everyone was silent, picturing Calder falling down a crack in the rocks, down the Cascade, or perhaps being swept downstream.

There was also the thought of a boy with no food and possibly no water for three whole days — not to mention no air.

Time, on that piece of land where people had hunted for so long, slowed to a crawl. Searchers were everywhere that night, armed with flashlights and machinery. People hunting people: The tools had changed, but the intensity had not.

▲ ▲ ▲ Petra could never remember, later, whether she had passed out from sheer terror or fallen asleep. The next thing she knew, after wedging herself tightly under the hedge, was the blinding light of a flashlight and a man's voice saying,

"Here she is, ma'am! It's the girl! Let's see what we have!"

And then she heard Mrs. Sharpe's reedy, "Wonderful! Do be careful, don't startle her!" coming from outside the maze.

Night had never looked as miraculous. After hearing that Tommy was safe and Calder was possibly being rescued, Petra swore that if Calder survived, nothing would ever, ever bother her again. Nothing.

And as she followed the police officer through the dark paths, she thought she would probably never set foot in another maze if she could help it. Not on purpose.

She practically floated across the lawn, her black hair matted with leaves, dirt, and bits of paper and garbage. The clouds were gone, the sky was awash with sparkling stars, and it was heavenly to be alive, to be walking, to be feeling the wind on her face.

And Mrs. Sharpe! How amazing that she was here! She stood near the wall of bushes, leaning heavily on her cane. Petra hurried over to say hello to her, then hesitated. Mrs. Sharpe held out her arms, and the two had a happy, unlikely hug. For a brief moment, dark tangles brushed across a white, biscuit-like bun.

Riding to the Cascade in the police car, Petra closed her eyes and sent silent messages to Calder: I'm here, Tommy's here, and you are, too. You are, you are! You'll be okay, I know it, I'm sure of it. I'm sending you a million wishes to help you be strong. Soon you'll be back in the world, in the beautiful night, in the wind.

It wasn't until the car stopped that Petra realized she had been holding Mrs. Sharpe's thin hand as she wished. She let go of it, and Mrs. Sharpe gave her a little nod, as if she knew exactly what was going on.

CHAPTER FORTY-TWO

▲ ▲ ▲ When Mrs. Sharpe and Petra arrived at the falls, they found Tommy sitting next to Walter Pillay on a rock. Calder's dad had his head down on his arms, which rested on his knees; Tommy's arm was draped over Walter's back, as if their roles had reversed, and one had become the adult and the other the child.

At the sound of Petra's voice, Tommy was on his feet, grinning. The two rushed into a hug that looked ridiculously awkward from the outside, but felt wonderful on the inside. Tommy received a bent-kneed shoulder crunch and what might have been a kiss on the ear. Petra got a foot-stomp and a huge belly-squeeze. Both kids had bruises and scrapes that hurt, but their hug was the most delicious thing either had felt in a long time. Or at least it *felt* like a long time; that day had been the longest day either one of them had ever known.

When they'd exchanged news, the group settled down to wait, including Pummy. An ambulance and a rescue team were parked on the bank. The police were clear about warning Walter Pillay that this latest exploration was only a possibility; if they didn't find his son that night it might, in fact, be a good sign. After all, the boy could walk out of the woods any second, much as the Calder sculpture had flown off a hay wagon on the bridge. The detective speaking attempted a dry laugh, but it was met only with a fragile, distracted silence. Walter Pillay turned the broken pentomino over and over in his fingers, as if touching each side and holding it from every angle might help.

Soon the earth-moving vehicle arrived and went to work, churning slowly and carefully. Rock by rock, the top of the falls was dismantled. Each time a boulder was lifted, water rushed under and around the hole, covering areas that had been dry for perhaps hundreds of years. Although this seemed precipitous and certainly dangerous, everyone agreed that waiting to dam and drain that part of the lake was not an option: Time was of the essence. If Calder was trapped inside the falls, every moment could count. Two divers in black rubber suits stood to one side of the vehicle, ready to jump in.

Tommy, watching from between Petra and Walter Pillay, squeezed his coin as hard as he could. Wish, he thought, wish. If this wish comes true, I'll be happy forever. Please. I'll never wish again.

No one but Petra knew about him finding this extraordinary coin, he'd gotten no glory, and suddenly that didn't matter. He didn't care if it was the oldest coin ever found, not if this worked.

In a quick motion, he tossed the coin as far as he could. Spinning and turning as it flew, it shot through the bright fan of emergency lights before vanishing into the dark waves of the lake.

No one said a word; everyone present understood.

In the next few minutes, as machinery ground and scraped against the boulders, a shower of coins flew, one after another, into the water. Mrs. Sharpe handed her coins to Tommy to throw. He also tossed Ms. Button's blue button. Petra threw everything she had: four pennies and a vitamin pill. Walter Pillay pitched every coin in both pockets, one at a time. Miss Knowsley threw all of her coins, and then the rest of the cracker crumbs. Even the police officers joined in.

Pling . . . ponk . . . blip . . . plink . . .

The patter of small disks falling on water was somehow comforting. Everyone was wishing.

▲ ▲ ▲ Just seconds after the last coin had been thrown, the two divers leaped forward, disappearing into a hole opened up by lifting a giant, trapezoidal rock. In the blink of an eye, Walter Pillay was in the water, lunging away from the grip of the policeman who jumped to restrain him.

The machine stopped moving and the engine was cut; time stopped; no one on the bank said a word. The only sounds were those of a man struggling through thigh-deep water, a man who didn't care if he slipped or fell.

The divers couldn't be seen, but low voices drifted back to the bank. Walter Pillay had, by then, scrambled up on the rocks behind them.

"Calder!" His voice was half scream and half shout, an eerie and terrible wail that ripped through the night. One of the divers stepped quickly up out of the hole, and in his arms was a boy.

The boy was limp, horribly limp, and as Walter Pillay clung to a boulder, suddenly unable to move, the diver leaped from rock to rock, rushing toward the ambulance on the bank.

Everyone watching was dead silent; as Calder's dad was helped into the ambulance with his boy, no one said a word.

The doors to the ambulance closed; emergency technicians disappeared into the back. After what felt to everyone watching like the longest few seconds in history, one of the nurses popped her head out a side window and shouted, "Radio the hospital that we're coming, quick! The lad's alive!"

CHAPTER FORTY-THREE

▲ ▲ ▲ Three days earlier:

It was dark, too dark to even imagine light. There was just the endless language of water, water splashing and gurgling and dripping and rushing. *Black, black, black* went a drip someplace to his right. He'd never realized how much the word fit what it sounded like: the flatness, the no-color, of dark water on dark stone. *Black, black, black.*

He wiggled his arms and legs. Everything was sore. Moving your body in total lack of light — was this like moving your body for the first time? And why couldn't he see?

One hand in front of his face, he sat up very, very slowly, ready at any moment to bump into something.

The slime on every surface, so slippery... Wasn't that why he had fallen down here? Had the slime become his mind? *Slip, slime, slip, slime*... there was a watery sound to every word. *Slip, slime, black, black... slip, slime, black, black.*

His hand hit rock an arm-length in front of him. The rock was cold and surprisingly dry. He pulled his hand back quickly, wiped it on his knee, and reached out again, *slowly, slowly*. The sounds of the words were as real as anything around him. He wanted to remember this later, the understanding that language blooms in the dark. Would he remember to tell Petra, who loved playing with words? He tried *white*, imagining brightness and the joy of being outside.

White, white, white — suddenly he could feel the lightness and the shimmer of midday, of a fat cloud overhead, the dart and dazzle of sun on water.

Maybe he'd hit his head, knocked himself out — he was quite sure he had — and now he had a crazy gift for language, a kind of mix-up of seeing and hearing. He tried another word, his eyes shut tight, although why bother? After all, shut and open were the same in here. *Tight shut, shut tight* — even the sounds of those two words were perfect for their meaning: *tight* had no air, no light, and *shut* was final, dreadful, closed.

He squeezed his eyes tight and, pressing on the lids, saw islands of red and maybe yellow. *Red,* the energetic sound of — of — suddenly he couldn't think of anything red, it seemed too crisp, too far away. Not blood — that had a wet and heavy sound to it that didn't fit. But the *Minotaur,* yes! He saw red suddenly, startling in its clarity and aliveness. *Red*: a clean, powerful sound. He knew why it was a favorite color for artists, suddenly he just knew it, in the way you feel how delicious food tastes when you're really hungry.

And here was *yellow, yellow* like a yell, a flash, a changeable shape. He listened to see if yellow was in the water surrounding him. Maybe in the rush behind the drips. Once in a while there was a spray sound, a kind of whoosh and fall of water . . . *yel-low, yel-low.*

Tommy would say he'd gone bananas, bananas without the peel, and that thought made him smile. Speaking of bananas, he knew he had fallen while walking next to the Cascade, a crazy fall. He'd slipped into some kind of secret space behind or under the rocks. He didn't remember losing his balance — strange.

He knew he'd been unconscious, and now had to find the strength to explore. *Yellow* — or was it *yelling* — might never be heard, he knew that, over the *black* of the water and the *red* of the rocks. Red? No red on rocks, but that was the hardness of the stone, the rolling R sounds. *R-r-red. Run. Roar. Red.*

Yellow, black, red, yellow, black, red . . . better to ignore *white*, the light. He found himself slipping into sleep again, even though he was sitting up. Just a little rest . . . He lowered himself back onto one bruised arm and lay on his side, cheek on his shoulder. *Cheek!* What a funny bird-word, like a hopping or a chirping. *Cheek, cheek!*

Then he heard something oddly unsoft, a crinkly sound coming from his pocket. Not his pentominoes — no, he'd know that sound anywhere. Not Miss Knowsley's key. The chocolate bars he'd bought after lunch! He reached his hand slowly into his pocket, feeling the joy of plastic wrappings. Pulling out one bar, he began to open it, slowly, carefully. As there was no light, no *white*, he couldn't risk dropping even one crumb. He felt around on the stone under his arm and realized it was flat, almost a floor. Better to roll onto his back and if the chocolate dropped, it would fall on top of him.

Cho-co-late, cho-co-late: the sound of sugar, of rectangles and their crunchy kindness. As he opened the top, the first whiff of chocolate was the best smell ever. It was blue sky, it was air, it was *cho-co-late*. The word was almost alive.

And the first bite! It was creamy and strong and more than delicious. It was a glimpse back into his old brain, his familiar mind. The sound language faded, and a more familiar way of thinking began to come back. Suddenly, the word *black* just sounded flat, like a word, and as he swallowed the last of the bar, he knew he'd fight to live.

Slowly, slowly, he got up on his knees. He stretched his arms over his head. Nothing. Just the steady rushing and dripping of the water. And then his fingers touched stone, recoiled, touched again. It was hard to reach out in the dark and not imagine what you might touch. What if this was a pirate hideaway and he touched an old foot, an eye socket, a jaw — a bunch of bones in cloth, a person who had been trapped in here hundreds of years ago? A hard, cold lump of fear settled into his guts, and he pushed the thought away, forcing himself to think of numbers. Numbers and shapes always helped.

He was dizzy, and sank back down. He'd work on another pentomino maze while he rested. But, no — mazes had dead ends, and he was in no mood for that. Maybe he'd play the Calder Game instead. He picked five of his favorite numbers and imagined them floating, their shapes connected by threads of light: 12 for his set of pentominoes and his age, 13 because other people were afraid of it but he wasn't, 3 for his family and also for his friendship with Petra and Tommy, 60 for the number of squares in every twelve-piece pentomino rectangle, and 41 because it was one of the coolest primes.

There, he did feel better. He could always rely on numbers.

Back up on his knees, he touched irregular boulders on all sides and tried to calculate dimensions. This space might be about the size of the coat closet at home. The stone was part dry, part wet. Some water was running over the rock, and water meant a crack. Did that mean a crack big enough to let in air? Maybe it was night outside, and when day came, he'd see light.

Light! It was hard to imagine. He thought if he saw light again, nothing could ever bother him. No problem would ever be a problem. He would be filled, forever, with the happiness of breathing and moving, of being alive. Nothing else.

Then he thought suddenly about the weight of stone. What if he had fallen into a tiny stone trap, a place with only a little air? No! He tried as hard as he could not to think about being buried alive.

He groped backward, in his thoughts, for that place of sound-language where the colors melted perfectly into sounds, and there was no past, no future. Only darkness, only sound.

Black, black, black went the water surrounding him, but the thought was no longer perfect, it was flat and bleak. *Black, black.*

▲ ▲ ▲ The next thing he knew, he was seeing something besides darkness. A shape. A shape! It was a round, hard edge of stone, and the loveliest line he'd ever seen. He rolled toward it, a fierce headache now throbbing. My brain pounding against my skull is just like me stuck in this stone room, he thought: *pound, pound, pound.* He touched the gray line, and it was wet. He licked his hand, and put it back, and again, and again. Then he pushed his fingers against the crack with the light, but all was water. No air. He could see light, but light behind water.

The tears welled up in his throat. He sank back down on the flat surface, trying to think. He rolled into a ball on his side and hugged his knees. His body was trying to comfort itself, keeping itself company, he realized. He patted his own shoulder and that felt good.

Maybe he'd fallen inside his name. His parents had told him that he'd been named for the famous artist, yes, and also that the word *calder* was very old, perhaps thousands of years old, and meant a stony stream, or fast-moving water over stone. Maybe he would just become his name, sink back into water and stone, and one day the rocks would move or wear down, and some bones, candy wrappers, and pieces of yellow plastic —

His pentominoes! He was up on his knees, fumbling in his pocket. He pulled out the L shape. Then he ran it carefully along the crack, slowly, pressing it as hard as he dared against the stone. A corner slid in and then stopped. He worked methodically, trying to fit the plastic and stone together in every possible combination. Whenever the pentomino seemed as though it might go in, he pushed with all of his strength, pushed until his arms shook.

Then he had another idea. He rolled over on his back and slammed the bottom of his sneaker against the pentomino as hard as he could. First he missed. Missed again. Then *snap*! The pentomino broke off, and he heard the clatter of plastic on stone. He felt around with his fingers. A small piece was still wedged in the crack.

He rested, his head now hammering mercilessly in his skull. He licked more water, this time directly off the rock beneath the crack.

He wondered how long his air would last.

Rest, he'd just rest for a few minutes. He pulled another pentomino out of his pocket. It was the W. W for wish, he thought to himself, and then wished with all his being that he could live. If this were a story, he realized, a story I was listening to or reading, I'd be angry. But I'm not.

Strange, he thought, he'd had so many unfamiliar feelings and sensations in this little stone room. The idea of using pentominoes to make mazes suddenly seemed crazy, almost cruel. Why would anyone want to get lost on purpose? He vowed, if he got out, to use his pentominoes only to help find things. He'd invent a maze with no dead ends.

He pushed the W into the crack and gave it another slam with his shoe, this time changing his angle. He thought his head would explode and he banged his knee hard, excruciatingly hard, but this time something wonderful happened: The W was gone. It was outside! He'd gotten it through the crack!

CHAPTER FORTY-FOUR

▲ ▲ ▲ By the next day, Calder knew they must be hunting for him. He could only hope, and then hope some more. *Hope.* The word had a lonely, clueless sound to it. What if no one living knew about this hidden room? And what if no one had seen him fall? But no: That wasn't possible.

Before his line of light melted back to dark, he had eaten the last chocolate bar and pounded all of his pentominoes into the crack in the rocks. Both knees were bleeding, and the soles of his feet ached from kicking against rock. Most of his pentomino pieces had broken — he'd heard the snap and felt the sharp shards of plastic scattered around him. But he was sure that the I had gotten through, and perhaps the long part of the T. And the W, yes, the W. Someone would see the yellow.

These pentominoes had done lots of thinking with him. He wondered how many of the sixty squares in his set had made it through the crack.

This was his first set, a set that a distant relative in London, someone who had since moved, had sent him for his twelfth birthday. They had helped him to put ideas and numbers together in a magical way; they had been a tool unlike anything he'd ever known. Numbers. Numbers seemed so safe now, and so far away.

By the time all was black again, he realized that it was warmer in his little cave. Not warmer, no, steamy. Airless.

His headache was becoming close to unbearable. He licked water off a rock and curled up again into a ball, whimpering now, and tried to picture the clean-edged pieces in the cool, dark water of the Cascade. If only they landed in a shallow pool, if only they weren't swept downstream, if only, if only.

Wish, wish, wish. Suddenly the word was beautiful, fluid and free in the water and stone and darkness that had become his world. *Wish,* like the sound of wings. His heart was pounding, and he felt the word beating in his veins: *Wish, wish, wish.*

CHAPTER FORTY-FIVE

▲ ▲ ▲ The hospital was buzzing the night the Boy was found, and the wind continued to blow, as if intent on pushing everyone involved into a new place.

Calder was in critical condition. He was severely dehydrated and very weak, having eaten nothing but his three chocolate bars for the last three days. Still unconscious, he was covered with scratches and bruises but didn't seem to have any serious injuries. His dad sat by his bed all night. He murmured to him, sang songs, and patted his hand, his head, his arm. Already thin, Calder was now a mere shadow, barely disturbing the layer of blankets that covered him.

Just down the corridor, Arthur Wish had slipped back into a comatose state. His aunt sat by the side of his bed chatting and knitting, and swore that he was listening to her. She told him the happy news about finding Calder — loudly, and many times over. She apologized for having been grumpy with him about the sculpture.

With neither Calder nor Arthur Wish able to talk, the questions swept through the hospital, and then through the town, like leaves in the wind.

Word spread at the post office when it opened the next morning: The American boy had been recovered, the man found under the willow was actually Posy Knowsley's nephew and the original owner of the *Minotaur*, and the sculpture itself was apparently lying beneath the bridge, at the bottom of the Queen Pool. Two local men had been arrested, and were being held by the police. They claimed an American had hired them to move the sculpture and had then abandoned them. No one knew who that American was. Americans! The town seemed to be full of them these days.

If anyone in Woodstock already knew the news, or knew more than that, they kept quiet about it.

Interestingly, the residents looked radiant that morning. There was whispering, however — at doorways, over fences, on street corners — and all remained careful not to speak around the police.

And then, just as Miss Knowsley got ready to leave the hospital and head back to feed Pummy and get some sleep, she was arrested.

Her eyes darting back and forth, her face pinched and angry, she was seen leaving the hospital in the back of a Thames Valley Police cruiser.

"The thanks I get for being a good auntie! The idea of spying in my house! How dare you? Justice, indeed! My Artie got kidnapped and coshed over the head, he did!"

The two police officers in the front seat slunk down like bad boys. Every third or fourth word, Miss Knowsley slapped the seat next to her. If she had had claws, the cushion would have been in shreds. If she'd had a tail, it would have been lashing.

CHAPTER FORTY-SIX

▲ ▲ ▲ Calder wasn't yet awake, but because of his age the doctors felt sure that he'd make a full recovery. They were more worried about the psychological trauma he might have suffered than about any long-term physical damage.

Walter Pillay had given permission for Tommy and Petra to stay in Calder's room, so that they, too, would be present when he opened his eyes. Calder's mom was so thrilled to hear the news about Calder that she could do nothing but laugh and cry, laugh and cry. She still wasn't able to get out of her hospital bed in Hyde Park, but doctors had told her that in time her cracked disk would heal. She spent all day admiring the clouds floating outside her window, thinking that they had never looked more extraordinary. She couldn't wait to have her husband and son home again.

Meanwhile, Woodstock murmurings continued in kitchens and on sidewalks throughout the town. News about Arthur Wish and his gift had spread. But what did it mean? And why all the secrecy?

Yes, the British police had been researching Mr. Wish, and had discovered the things Walter Pillay had found. But were Art Wish's good deeds just a cover for something darker? And why exactly did he like that troublemaker artist Banksy? A copy of Banksy's book *Wall and Piece* was found in Art Wish's hotel room.

Until Calder awoke, no one knew if Mr. Wish's accident had anything to do with Calder's. Was Mr. Wish, as Walter Pillay suspected, the man Calder had been shaking hands with in the square? Why were they both near the Cascade that day? Had a third person — or possibly a group of people — tried to murder them both?

Banksy, of course, could not be reached.

The police also wondered how much Miss Knowsley really knew about her wealthy American nephew. Could she possibly have been kicking up a fuss about the *Minotaur* as a screen for his activities? Could he have offered her money in return for local camouflage or help? The police had found scribbles on a pad in her kitchen, drawings of the top of the Cascade and a gap in the rocks. Had these been done the night Calder was found, as she claimed, or several days earlier? And what did the money signs that trailed down the side of the page mean? Was it only that she was worried about paying the gas bills that winter, as she'd told the police? Or had she played a part in helping her nephew to get rid of the boy?

Perhaps Calder had stumbled on undercover activity of some kind. Maybe someone needed him to have that accident.

Even if Miss Knowsley had helped her nephew without realizing the depth of her involvement, she was a suspect. At least until the boy, and hopefully her nephew, awoke and vindicated her.

Everyone was waiting for Calder to speak.

▲ ▲ ▲ Petra, Tommy, and Walter Pillay were playing a game of cards at the foot of Calder's bed when he awoke.

"Hi, you guys," he said slowly, his voice barely a whisper. "Hi."

The response was thunderous and bouncy and tearful. Calder apologized over and over to his dad, and kept saying, "I can't believe you're here!" to Petra and Tommy.

Although a nurse tried to keep him quiet, a member of the police was allowed in, and Calder shared the bare bones of the story:

He and Arthur Wish had been talking by the *Minotaur*. Yes, he'd introduced himself to Calder. Mr. Wish, after seeing Calder's mazes and listening to his thoughts about the Calder Game, then explained what he was doing. He told Calder he liked the idea of the boy playing a part.

He'd identified himself as the collector who had given the *Minotaur* to Woodstock, but said that he was troubled by how much the residents seemed to dislike it. He explained that he'd been listening to their comments for a couple of weeks, and had decided to do something about it, something that hopefully would be a success-ful surprise. He'd hired some men to move the sculpture the following night.

He invited Calder to help him decide on a possible new home for the work of art. Would he take a walk through Blenheim Park with him the next day? Art Wish said he hoped that seeing the *Minotaur* in the park, with more space around it, would make the residents of Woodstock get to know it in a more accepting way. Calder loved the idea.

He remembered that he and Art Wish had been walking near the top of the Cascade when Calder had slipped. Or had he stepped on something that moved beneath him? He really wasn't sure. Falling was the last thing he remembered before waking up in his tiny stone prison.

The detective who'd been listening and taking notes looked up. "Didn't feel a push, did you?" he asked. Calder frowned.

"No," he said slowly. "I wasn't pushed. I fell."

"Whose idea was it to walk all the way to the Cascade?" the detective asked.

Calder thought for a moment. "I'm not sure. I think it was Art Wish's idea — but we both wanted to go there."

The detective nodded his head, as if to say, "Just what I thought."

▲ ▲ ▲ Over the next five days, Calder stayed in the hospital, slowly regaining his strength. Arthur Wish remained in a comatose state.

Miss Knowsley was allowed to return to her home on Alehouse Lane, much to Pummy's delight, but was kept under house arrest. The police felt it was wise until they could corroborate Calder's story.

The name of the young girl in black was Georgia Rip. She brought Miss Knowsley groceries and was permitted by the police to stay on in the house. Her father, Nashton Rip, was one of the two stonemasons currently under arrest for stealing the sculpture. The other three men hadn't turned themselves in, and Mr. Rip and his partner still wouldn't supply their names. Both Tommy and Petra had told the police that they'd heard people moving around in the park that night, in the woods and by the maze, but that didn't help in identifying the other thieves.

The fact that Miss Knowsley was both Art Wish's aunt and Nashy Rip's cousin didn't improve her case in the eyes of the police. She and Pummy and Georgia had all of their meals at the kitchen table, and Miss Knowsley, who tended to be emotional at the best of times, frequently burst into tears or thumped the table with her fist.

She still felt the Americans were to blame. "Poisoned my Artie, that's what they've done — poisoned his brain many years ago!"

She refused to believe he'd done anything wrong, and said many rude things about the Thames Valley Police. She would NEVER speak with them again. "I already knew they were not to be trusted," she muttered to Pummy. "They'll pay for this, they will!"

"*Yeow!*" Pummy chimed in.

All three enjoyed quantities of bacon that week. Georgia Rip, who had been living alone with her father since the death of her mother two years before, seemed happy to be around Miss Knowsley; her father, moody and angry much of the time, wasn't an easy man. The young policeman watching the house marveled at all the delicious smells coming from the kitchen. He once knocked on the back door in order to compliment Miss Knowsley on her cooking, hoping to be asked in for a bite. No such luck: The door was slammed in his face. The young girl later peeked out at him from behind a curtain, as if he were someone to avoid.

Even the black cat had glared at him, with his one unforgettable eye.

▲ ▲ ▲ Calder, Petra, and Tommy did lots of things to pass the time.

First, they did a great deal of talking. His voice still hoarse, Calder described what had happened while he was lost — the strange way words shifted in his brain, as if they came alive in all that darkness.

"It was like my mind borrowed part of Petra's mind," Calder said.

"Hey! That happened to me, too," Tommy added. "I started thinking like Petra last night, while I was alone in the park, and the whole time we've been looking for you, numbers have been popping up in the weirdest ways. You know, like your pattern stuff."

"And I've been problem-solving like both of you guys, rearranging letters and symbols like Calder, and also feeling braver because of Tommy," Petra added. "It's as if we're not in our familiar places anymore."

Although he said nothing about it, Calder was amazed at how relaxed Petra and Tommy seemed with each other. What had happened while they were alone together? He knew it wasn't a good idea to ask, but he hoped this would last. It was new for the three of them, and made doing things together much, much more fun. The balance had changed, and he was no longer stuck in the middle.

The three of them also talked about the power of wishing. Tommy told Calder about his incredible find, the 1752 coin, and about how he'd thrown it into the Queen Pool. He felt sure that the coin had made a difference. He also mentioned the fate of the Button's blue button.

Calder thanked his old friend. He knew how much Tommy's treasures meant to him. He also thanked Petra for all her looking and thinking and wishing.

"Wishes can be so strong," Petra mused. "It just doesn't make sense that Mr. Wish is a bad man. With his WISH-WISH message, he planted the idea of wishes in everyone's head."

"Plus, he dreamed up the Calder Game, which has been a giant gift to thousands of people around the world," Walter Pillay added. "And he started the Free Art: Share It! foundation, which has given so much to all of us, but to children in particular."

"That's a funny name for a foundation, isn't it?" Calder asked.

"I like it," Tommy said. "Art *should* be free."

"It's almost as if he knew that he, Art, might be losing his freedom," Petra said.

Calder picked up a bedside pad of paper and a pencil and began writing things. "Hey," he said after several moments. "HEY! If you write the name of his foundation in capital letters, you'll see that the letters in SHARE IT spell out ART WISH, if you turn the E into a sideways W. That's the kind of thing I would do. I *knew* I liked that guy!"

"The man likes games," Walter Pillay remarked.

▲ ▲ ▲ When the news about Arthur Wish's anonymous gift to Woodstock and subsequent injury hit the American newspapers, there was a renewed rush to visit the Calder exhibit in Chicago, and a new crop of people threw themselves into the Calder Game. Hearing about Art Wish's idea of making an idea-mobile by giving Calder sculptures to five communities in the world had started people thinking. Other people gave valuable things, and posted mobiles made from the idea of their gifts.

The museum reported that the submissions in the Take Five room had become so marvelous and meaningful that they were planning a separate exhibit, after Alexander Calder's mobiles were taken down, of ordinary people's idea-mobiles.

There was a plan to make a citywide Chicago exhibit of Take Five mobiles that spring and summer, posting large versions of individual mobiles on buses, on street displays, and on the sides of buildings.

Americans didn't seem concerned at all about the news that Art Wish had possibly stolen his own gift in order to relocate it. Why not? After all, he wasn't *really* stealing it.

The British police were less forgiving, although they reluctantly admitted that they didn't consider Arthur Wish's actions to be a crime.

They were also miffed when a fresh piece of graffiti turned up by Trafalgar Fountain in front of the National Gallery in London. It said, in stenciled yellow letters:

FREE ART WISH
WISH FREE ART
ART WISH FREE

FREE ART WISH
WISH FREE ART
ART WISH FRE
FREE WIS

ART FREE WISH
FREE WISH ART
WISH ART FREE

Encircling these six lines were versions of the WISH-WISH stencil, with the Is crossing to form an X, just as they had in Woodstock. The WISH signs looked like stars floating around the longer message.

All day, coins flew by the dozens into the fountain. London street-cleaners were forbidden to get rid of the graffiti, at least for the time being.

When the *Minotaur* was retrieved, very carefully, from the bottom of the Queen Pool, most of Woodstock crowded around to watch. And, one by one, the locals helped: Before the sculpture was loaded into a waiting truck, hands reached out to remove pondweed or brush off a gob of mud. Townspeople of all ages followed the truck as it rumbled slowly back toward Woodstock and the town square. Once the sculpture was unloaded, examined by experts, and pronounced to be in perfect condition, many volunteers worked to clean and polish it. Others brought sandwiches and cookies and tea. Somehow, everyone knew where they wanted the sculpture to go, and it was soon back in place, next to the WISH-WISH stencil. Surrounded by lots of stone and a scattering of leaves, the *Minotaur* shone in the fall sunshine.

"Marvelous we never dredged leaves from the pool," one voice remarked. "Nice soft cushion."

"Marvelous it survived the adventure," said another, nodding.

"Yes, the wishes all worked," yet another voice said, as if the whole thing had been planned.

Strange events were happening in both the United States and England, and they clearly had a great deal to do with one man, a man who still wasn't able to speak.

CHAPTER FORTY-SEVEN

▲ ▲ ▲ While they waited for Calder to gain strength and hoped that Art Wish would recover, an odd foursome traveled back and forth to the hospital in Woodstock every day.

Sometimes the group dozed or read, and sometimes they all played the Calder Game.

Among the mobiles that were taped to Calder's hospital wall was one called *Tricks of Time*, made by Mrs. Sharpe; one titled *We Five,* by Petra; a *Treasure* mobile by Tommy; and one called *Word Equations,* about the sound-ideas Calder remembered from his days inside the Cascade. Walter Pillay made a mobile from drawing the shapes of the five largest rocks that were so carefully moved to reveal his son. He titled it *Rocks*, and the outlines he drew on paper looked oddly like shapes Alexander Calder would have loved. Doctors and nurses watched the collection grow, and then asked if they could add some of their own.

"How about a new code?" Tommy asked Calder one day.

Calder smiled. "I've had an idea for a while. A really unusual code: You could make a list of twenty-six shapes that Alexander Calder used in his mobiles, and give a letter of the alphabet to each one. How's that?"

"Fabulous!" Petra said, and immediately began working on the list. The other four added on to it. Mrs. Sharpe called a bookstore in Oxford and ordered an art book with photographs of many of Alexander Calder's mobiles. She also ordered a surprise for Calder, delivered in the same package: a new set of pentominoes, complete with its own wooden box.

Calder whooped with delight.

"It's beyond cool, Mrs. Sharpe!" he crowed, and even managed to give her an awkward, double-bony hug.

"Don't strangle me, boy!" she said, obviously pleased. She settled back in her chair, patting her bun into place and studying the pictures in the Calder book.

While Calder played around with his new pentominoes that afternoon, the other four made

up the list of twenty-six. Here is what they came
up with:

"There!" Mrs. Sharpe waved a piece of paper
triumphantly in Calder's direction. "We've written something in Calder Code. Can you read it?"

Calder puzzled over the string of shapes, which looked more like weird jewelry than a language. His finger moved back and forth across the page:

"I will!" He grinned. "It's great, you guys!" Amazingly, Mrs. Sharpe didn't correct him. She didn't even seem to mind being included as one of the guys.

"Wonderful, just wonderful. I love a challenge," she was heard muttering.

Calder handed over a tidy rectangle he'd drawn while they were working on the Calder Code, with directions. "It's a pentomino maze, but one with no dead ends," he said triumphantly. "I'll never make anything with dead ends again."

Calder's maze was really a game, and he wrote out these instructions:

"Here is a game board and a sample game. On this one, the score is six," Calder explained.

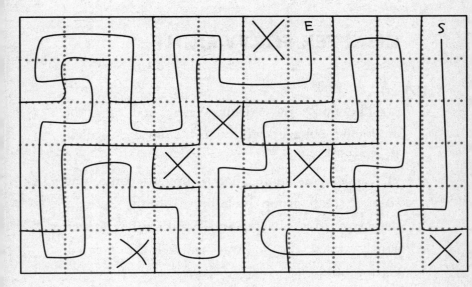

That evening, the day before Calder was discharged from the hospital, Arthur Wish opened his eyes.

CHAPTER FORTY-EIGHT

▲ ▲ ▲ "Boy."

The nurse by Arthur Wish's bed rang the emergency buzzer wildly. "He's awake! Quick! Bring the Boy!"

Calder was more than happy to come, and soon a small group including Tommy, Petra, a detective, Mrs. Sharpe, and Walter Pillay moved slowly down the hallway toward the Critical Care room.

Art Wish looked blank until he saw Calder. A tiny smile flickered across his face. "Yes," he said. "Yes."

And then the shadow-thin boy and the man with the bandaged head sat together until the man gained enough strength to speak. It was clear that just the sight of Calder made things better; the man seemed immensely relieved.

When Art Wish was finally able to talk, he told this story:

He had noticed Calder by himself in town, and then making his pentomino mazes in the

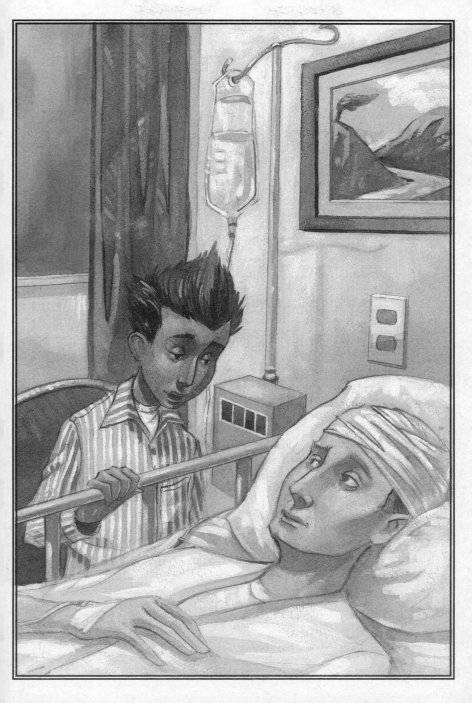

graveyard. When the boy came into the Lyon Tea Shop, ordered a sandwich, and gave the name "Calder," Art Wish knew they should talk. Calder then forgot his maze diagrams, and Art Wish picked them up, planning to return them — their meeting seemed almost inevitable. Recognizing that these drawings were the work of an enterprising thinker, Art Wish decided to see if the American boy would share his reactions to the *Minotaur*.

Art Wish went on, his face suddenly growing sad, "You see, I was feeling quite confused. I'd given the *Minotaur* to Woodstock just about the time the show in Chicago opened in September, but hadn't visited it yet. Then, while sitting in the exhibit shortly after the *Minotaur* was installed, I had an idea: I'd make a giant mobile by giving five Calder sculptures from my own collection to five communities in the world. You know, with the thought of making great art available for anyone to enjoy. I would only pick pieces the artist had named after creatures. The *Minotaur* would be the first part of this unusual mobile.

"I was very excited and rushed home, went through the names on all of my large Calder sculptures, picked four to give away and four wonderful places in the world to receive them, and then returned to the Take Five room several days later and hung my idea. The next day I got on a plane for England. I came directly to Woodstock.

"Part of my plan was to record local people's reactions to the art. I wanted to be sure that each piece was in the right place. And I wanted to document what I did, kind of like the British artist Banksy. I also wanted to remain anonymous. I thought I'd get far more done if I didn't have a name. I was thinking I might even, one day, make a book from it."

The detective nodded, his mouth turning down in a *well-maybe* curve.

"Terrific idea, your anonymous mobile made of donated Calder sculptures," Mrs. Sharpe said in a stern but very kind tone. "Shows great vision."

"Thank you," Art Wish said quietly. "Anyway,

I then arrived here, and was disturbed and saddened to hear all the negative feelings about the *Minotaur*. Even my aunt hated it. I was interested in what children thought, especially, but there weren't many children around. I tried to speak with a young girl who seemed intrigued by the *Minotaur*, but she ran away. I really didn't know what to do. And then I met Calder here —" Art Wish paused and gave Calder another smile, "— and I knew he'd be a help in solving this puzzle.

"I'd already made plans to have the *Minotaur* moved, but I wasn't yet sure where to relocate it. It seemed like the perfect solution, to involve a creative kid. So off we went."

Here Art Wish had to rest. When he felt able to speak again, he said softly, "My big mistake was to remember. I'd spent one wonderful summer with my aunt here, as a kid, and never forgot the Cascade. As a boy, I'd heard the story about a secret platform in those rocks, and always dreamed of finding some part of it. I thought maybe I'd be allowed to stay longer in Woodstock if I did. You know — as a kind of local hero." He smiled.

"Well, once we got into the park, I told Calder the old story. He was excited, and suggested we look at the spot, possibly even as a place to relocate the sculpture. And there we were, walking along the edge of the rocks, and he suddenly seemed to lose his balance, stumble, and fall between two boulders. He disappeared. I've never witnessed anything like it! He absolutely disappeared. There was a horrible rumbling sound, like rocks rubbing, and he was gone. Gone! Scariest thing I've ever seen."

Mr. Wish's eyes filled with tears. "I'm so sorry," he said to Calder.

Calder shook his head, as if to say there was no need to be sorry.

Mr. Wish closed his eyes, but kept talking. "And then everything went wrong. My cell phone wasn't working. There was no one around, and I ran along the bank to get help. As you know, it's quite a distance to the gates, and I was panicky. Maybe I wasn't careful. I must have slipped and hit my head on a rock, but I don't remember doing that. I only remember a flash of terrible pain and then the next thing I knew, I was in the hospital here."

"Bad injury on the back of your head," the detective said. "Looked more like someone hit you with a blackjack, then tried to hide you in that dense grove of bamboo. You're lucky to be alive."

"*Hmm*," Art Wish said, his expression troubled.

"And what about the WISH-WISH sign?" Walter Pillay chimed in.

"Oh, that!" Mr. Wish gave another weak smile. "I'm a big Banksy fan. Maybe I was just adding a little touch of Banksy to the picture. I made the stencil, and asked the men who moved the *Minotaur* that night to paint it on."

"You said 'men' just now," the detective interjected. "Happen to remember their names?"

Art Wish shook his head. "I only spoke directly to one, a really big fellow, and as I didn't give him *my* name, I couldn't exactly pressure him for *his*."

Walter Pillay nodded. "Yes, I understand."

"I don't," the detective muttered.

"I do," Calder said. "Understand, I mean. I like all the stuff you've done. This has been an awful experience, but a kind of wonderful one, too." Tommy and Petra were nodding.

"I think we all see one another differently than we did before this happened," Calder said. "All of us."

"Yes, the wind came up —" Mrs. Sharpe began. She paused.

"And changed us all," Petra said softly.

CHAPTER FORTY-NINE

▲ ▲ ▲ While Arthur Wish was recovering, the other five stayed in Woodstock for another two days, enjoying the town and lots of friendly smiles and pats on the back while all the police business was wrapped up. Walter Pillay was treated to a number of free ales, and Mrs. Sharpe to some delicious sherry.

Miss Knowsley was all fluff and flutter, having been released, but made a point of snubbing every police officer in Woodstock. She even crossed streets and rushed out of stores in order to avoid them, as if she might catch a terrible disease. Pummy became even fatter, if that was possible. He enjoyed a number of large, jolly meals in the dining room at Miss Knowsley's over the next week, meals that included the two Pillays, Mrs. Sharpe, Tommy, and Petra. Calder felt he owed Pummy a great deal, and lots of roast pheasant and mutton found its way under the table.

Mrs. Knowsley introduced her young cousin Georgia Rip to the group, and was very glad she had.

Calder gasped when he saw her. "Bird Girl!" he blurted.

She frowned and said formally, "My name is Georgia, like the American painter Georgia O'Keeffe."

Over the course of a meal, she began to relax. By dessert — treacle pudding — she was talking. She told the group that she'd been drawn to the *Minotaur* from the moment she saw it. She loved painting and sketching. Her mother had been an artist, although not a famous one, and had insisted on her daughter's name. Her dad, who felt art was for dreamers, didn't want Georgia to become an artist. When she became fascinated with the Calder sculpture, he tried to prevent her from seeing it anymore. She began sneaking around.

"The stuff of legends," Mrs. Sharpe said quietly.

Georgia nodded, surprising Mrs. Sharpe. She went on, "And then I was in the Lyon Tea Shop one day, and you came in, Calder, and I couldn't believe someone else might have an artist's name also. I wanted to talk to you, but then I had to pretend I wasn't interested, because I thought my dad was watching me. He'd already decided he didn't like you, probably because you're American. My poor dad," Georgia said, frowning again. "He didn't mean anything dreadful to happen — he just got carried away. I know he wanted the best for me."

Petra, Tommy, and Calder all felt sorry for Georgia, and tried to make her comfortable. She was several years older than they were, but didn't look it. Straw-thin, she had a nervous habit of rubbing the toe of one shoe against the heel of the other while she spoke.

The four kids settled at one end of Miss Knowsley's dining room table, and Calder, Tommy, and Petra explained the Calder Game. Georgia had no idea that the artist Calder had made sculptures that move, and she whispered,

"Brilliant! Just brilliant!" The three friends showed her some of their recent mobiles, and soon Georgia was making her own. The first mobile she showed them was a series of five views of the *Minotaur*, sketched as if the giant sculpture were floating in space. She worked with confident, clean strokes, as if she could spin the structure in her mind.

"Wow," Calder said. "You're good at this."

Walter Pillay, watching her, asked, "*Did* you take the picture of Calder and Art Wish in the square, the one I asked you about a few days ago? It's okay if the answer is yes."

Georgia shook her head. "That was my mother's camera. I use it to see. I've never had any film in it; my dad wouldn't allow it."

Tommy asked her where she'd learned to draw.

"I've had lots of time on my own, and I guess it's in my blood. My mother wasn't well for most of my childhood, and couldn't really teach me."

Tommy nodded, thinking about his own abilities as a finder. His dad, who had been gone since he was a baby, had been trained as an archaeologist. Spotting treasures was just something Tommy knew how to do — no one had taught him.

Petra then asked Georgia if she'd like to collaborate on a word-picture mobile, and soon their heads were together as they stirred sketches with words, crossed things out in excitement, rewrote, re-drew, laughed with delight, and added scribbled notes and arrows.

Tommy and Calder had a glimpse of verbs (*glimmer, glisten, gallop*) interspersed with peeking faces. In between, lines of irregular bubbles filled with adjectives and creatures (*slippery, shining, snake, snail*) drifted across the page. It all seemed quite strange to the boys, who then had the same thought.

"Alexander Calder's studio," Tommy said.

"Right." Calder nodded. "The best inventions are a mess while being invented."

"Thanks," Petra said, but didn't look insulted.

Georgia Rip only smiled.

Mrs. Sharpe remarked to Miss Knowsley,

"Unusual girl, your cousin. Reminds me of myself at that age."

"Really!" Miss Knowsley chirped.

Mrs. Sharpe then invited Georgia to visit Chicago that winter, provided that Miss Knowsley agreed. The elderly American said she had a big house, lots of art books, and plenty of time. Calder, Petra, and Tommy urged Georgia to come, telling her there was much to see and explore.

Georgia beamed, thanked Mrs. Sharpe, and said she'd think about it. Walter Pillay, remembering the jumpy creature of several days before, didn't think she even looked like the same girl.

▲ ▲ ▲ The people of Woodstock were developing a tender and newly proud relationship with their *Minotaur*, and Miss Knowsley even described the sculpture as a "wonder" to her nephew. There was a general feeling that the *Minotaur* had saved the boy by leaping into the Queen Pool and creating a wave that exposed the puzzle piece. After all, Woodstock residents had always lived

with large creatures, mazes, and legend, and believed that nothing of value happened without connection to the past. As soon as the *Minotaur* came alive, joining the realm of symbol and story, it was accepted into the community and all bad feelings forgotten.

Miss Knowsley ordered new key rings for her house, with the inscription: *Visit Woodstock, Home of Kings and Minotaurs*.

"Never mind that there's only one," she remarked lightly to anyone who would listen. "Maybe my Artie will find us another!"

From his hospital bed, where he lay quietly for several weeks, Arthur Wish gave instructions not to prosecute the men who moved the sculpture on that fateful night. He wanted to pay them for their trouble and worries, and planned to ignore any other plans they might have made. Nashy Rip and his accomplice, however, did go to prison for trying to steal the priceless work of art for themselves, and for trying to talk the police into giving them a reward.

Later that year, Art Wish bought an old stone cottage in the center of town, and became a familiar face in the community. He gladly helped his aunt with the upkeep on their old family house, and Miss Knowsley was now able to have guests only when she wanted, and to knit and rock and chat for hours on end. Georgia now lived with Miss Knowsley, and was soon seen wearing a lovely red sweater. Mrs. Sharpe had arranged for her to have art lessons, and left her the Alexander Calder art book she had bought while Calder was in the hospital.

Georgia cut up some of her old clothes and sewed a number of black mice for Pummy. She tied some of Miss Knowsley's red wool around each mouse's neck, and ran Pummy around the house to give him extra exercise. Pummy became hungrier than ever.

The other four sculptures that were a part of Mr. Wish's original mobile were installed around the world, and Arthur Wish spent several months traveling and watching and thinking. He was now very careful about how and where

Alexander Calder's work was introduced to any community.

Sadly, the graffiti message in Trafalgar Square was scrubbed away, and its maker remained a mystery.

And Banksy, wherever he was, stayed quiet about the Calder Game.

CHAPTER FIFTY

▲ ▲ ▲ When Calder, Petra, and Tommy walked into their seventh-grade classroom in Chicago, a barely recognizable version of the Button rushed over and gave them a hug.

"Oh, it's so wonderful to see you three!" she beamed, clearly meaning what she said.

Their mouths open, the three kids stared. The classroom looked completely different. All of the desks had been pushed into clusters; there were no rows. And the walls were covered with mobiles — every inch but the windows had mobiles of all sizes and colors, all on paper. It was a miraculous collage of ideas, a joyful mishmash of talkative colors and shapes.

Ms. Button threw out her arms. "Welcome home," she said. She was wearing blue jeans, to their amazement, and her hair looked like Ms. Hussey had gotten to it.

"What happened?" Petra managed to ask.

Ms. Button thought for a moment, her head on one side. "Alexander Calder happened," she said slowly. "And Arthur Wish. And the three of you."

"Amazing," was all Calder could say, and he ran his fingers through his new set of wooden pentominoes.

There was no doubt about it: The wind had changed, blowing them all into a new alignment. The people involved all saw things differently; the city of Chicago saw things differently; much of Woodstock saw things differently; and things were still moving.

How had it all happened? Where had it started? It was hard to say.

The mobiles had begun with Alexander Calder, of course, but this was larger than any one man or his art. The Calder Game had taken on a life of its own.

And was this really a game?

Maybe, but no one who played it was ever quite the same.

AUTHOR'S NOTE

▲ ▲ ▲ A number of mobiles were left behind when the five Americans went home that fall. In the Woodstock Hospital reception area, these were seen recently, neatly pinned to a bulletin board:

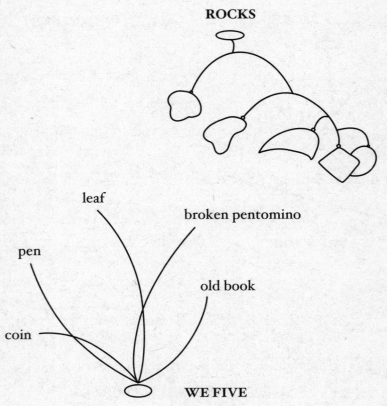

ROCKS

leaf

broken pentomino

pen

old book

coin

WE FIVE

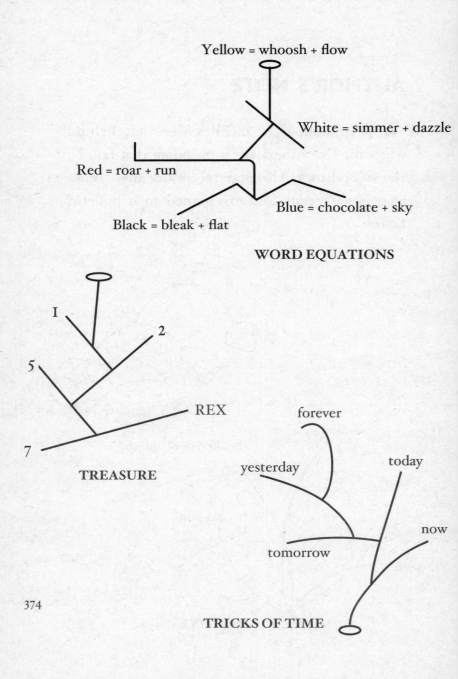

Yellow = whoosh + flow

White = simmer + dazzle

Red = roar + run

Blue = chocolate + sky

Black = bleak + flat

WORD EQUATIONS

1

2

5

REX

7

TREASURE

forever

yesterday

today

now

tomorrow

TRICKS OF TIME

Another mobile was found on a crinkled piece of paper next to the Blenheim Park wall. It was kept by a shy and eccentric Woodstock resident, someone who rarely left home. This person tucked the mobile in a drawer, since it looked as if it should remain hidden:

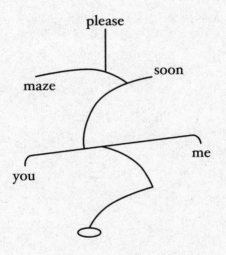

After all, what if Rosamund had sent it to Henry, or Henry to Rosamund?

As everyone knew, Woodstock had its old secrets, and those secrets, if stumbled upon, were not to be told.

AUTHOR'S WHISPER

▲ ▲ ▲ The *Minotaur* is an invented combination of several large sculptures that Alexander Calder made in the 1950s. If you look at some of Calder's many freestanding sculptures, or stabiles, as he called the ones without movement, you will be able to imagine it.

▲ ▲ ▲ The mobiles in this book fall into two categories: ones made by Calder, and ones inspired by him. There are several that occur in landscape (think primary colors), others created of people and by people, ones drawn and painted and printed, and a handful that consist of ideas. Perhaps you'll recognize still another kind of mobile, one no one else has yet identified.

▲ ▲ ▲ The Jean-Paul Sartre quote on page 10 was taken from *Calder's Universe*, by Jean Lipman, page 261. She references the famous preface

Jean-Paul Sartre wrote in French for the Galerie Louis Carre exhibition in Paris in 1946. There have been several translations into English.

▲ ▲ ▲ Pentominoes are real. They are a math tool, and look like this:

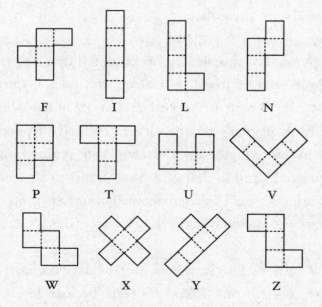

Thousands of different rectangles can be made with this set of twelve pieces.

▲ ▲ ▲ Woodstock is very real, and so is Blenheim Palace and its park. All of the history and geography is accurate except for one street name, one garden name, and the placement of several invented businesses. Hyde Park, Calder and Tommy and Petra's neighborhood in Chicago, is also real.

▲ ▲ ▲ Banksy is real and lives in England. I want to thank him for inspiring so many people, including me.

▲ ▲ ▲ In his illustrations, Brett Helquist has hidden, in Calder code, eleven letters. As in a mobile, the letters float and drift. Once you have collected them all, you can arrange them in an order that will spell out a message. The letters appear in a pattern of fives.

AFTER WORDS™

BLUE BALLIETT'S
The Calder Game

ILLUSTRATED BY BRETT HELQUIST

CONTENTS

After Words™ guide by Erin Black

About the Author

Blue Balliett's books reflect her interest in seemingly unexplainable events and her passion to ask questions.

Growing up in New York City, she loved the freedom of city life and exploring its wonders — the Metropolitan Museum of Art, the Guggenheim Museum, the Frick Collection, and Central Park. Blue took public transportation to school and around the city, and discovered early that every crowded bus or train is packed with mystery and drama — she learned that stories are everywhere, and there is always something to wonder about.

After graduating from Brown University with a degree in art history, Blue moved to Nantucket Island in order to write. There she worked as a grill cook, a waitress, a researcher of old houses, and an art gallery director while she wrote two books of ghost stories, stories collected by interviewing people who lived on the island.

When her children started school, the family moved to Chicago, to the neighborhood known as Hyde Park (sound familiar?), and she began teaching third grade at the University of Chicago Laboratory Schools. One year she and her class decided to figure out what art was about. They were looking for ways to feel comfortable thinking about art, and the real questions art historians live with. They came up with countless questions, visited many museums in the city, and had scavenger hunts that resulted in setting off a number of alarms — by mistake, of course.

These experiences were part of the inspiration behind

Chasing Vermeer, *The Wright 3*, and *The Calder Game*. Blue also wrote the books to explore the ways in which kids perceive connections between supposedly unrelated events and situations, connections that many adults often miss. Is a coincidence really just a coincidence? Before she wrote *The Calder Game*, Blue was on a book tour in England when she and her husband stopped in a small town called Woodstock. As she told the *Chicago Tribune* in an interview, she looked at the empty town square and thought, "What would happen if they had a fantastic sculpture in their square? What would happen to the town?"

To answer this question, Blue found herself thinking of two artists she admired — the famous sculptor Alexander Calder and the mysterious street artist Banksy. She immersed herself in their work and also returned to Woodstock, this time with a mystery on her mind.

When she started writing *Chasing Vermeer*, Blue chose to work at a desk in her family's laundry room. Now, even though her books have been bestsellers and have been translated into more than twenty-five languages, she *still* writes in the laundry room, letting her characters wander the neighborhood and travel the world, looking for clues and making those unexpected connections.

About the Illustrator

Brett Helquist was born in a very small town in Arizona where there was nothing to see for miles around, except a lot of red dirt. With not much else for him and his six sisters to do, he learned to use his imagination. That and his discovery of the newspaper comic strips — his favorite was *Alley Oop* — was what started him off drawing. As a kid, he spent many hours dreaming of creating his own comic strips.

When Brett was about eleven years old, his family moved to Utah, where there was a lot to do. He became interested in fishing, hiking, and camping, and didn't think very much about being an artist anymore. He had decided he wanted to be a scientist in order to better understand the world around him.

Then while in college at Brigham Young University, Brett started to think about art again. He began as an engineering major, but soon realized it was not the right choice. He decided to take some time off and headed for Taiwan. There he stumbled into work illustrating textbooks and a year later went back to school to study illustration. From that moment on, he knew what he wanted to do.

Soon after graduation he moved to New York City, where he still lives with his wife and daughter. Before becoming a full-time illustrator, Brett worked as a graphic designer. His illustrations have appeared in magazines, newspapers, picture books, and novels. As an artist, Brett tries to be observant, to look carefully, and to discover the beautiful and amazing things all around him.

Q&A with Blue Balliett

Q: *Your appreciation of Alexander Calder's work comes through strongly in* The Calder Game. *What do you think is the appeal of his sculptures — to both kids and adults?*

A: There is something deeply satisfying about his sculpture that is hard to explain — I've been looking at it for over forty years, and I still don't really understand where the "just right" feeling comes from. His work is a crazy bundle of opposites. It's playful and unpretentious — accessible to all ages — yet unpredictable, asymmetrical, graceful, balanced. There is something oddly alive about these metal constructions, something that doesn't seem to depend on any formula or set of ingredients. Hmm, perhaps it's magic.

Q: *What do you want readers to come away with when they read* The Calder Game?

A: Lots of questions that weren't in their minds before they picked up the book, such as: Can life itself be seen as a mobile? How does context change how you see, whether you're looking at art or yourself or another person? What does it mean to be "foreign"? How can art be freed? Does it need to be freed?

Q: *What type of research did you do for* The Calder Game?

A: I visited and stayed in Woodstock, England, three times, read lots on the history of the town and on Blenheim, ate every kind of Cadbury chocolate, read many books about Alexander Calder and saw as much of his work as possible, read as much about Banksy and his art as I could find, and did a ton of research on hedge mazes, including getting lost in a number of massive, prickly ones in England. Research is a great excuse for having adventures.

Q: *Why did you choose a small town in England as the setting for* The Calder Game?

A: After completing a book tour in England a couple of years ago, my husband and I rented a car and drove around the Cotswolds. We stumbled on Woodstock, and suddenly I knew that Calder, Petra, and Tommy should go there, too. I hadn't planned to write a book set outside of the United States, but Woodstock had a maze of just the right size, and a small community that kids could navigate on their own. It just felt perfect.

Q: *Had you always planned to write a third book about Calder, Petra, and Tommy?*

A: No, I didn't plan these three mysteries way ahead of time. For each of the three, I've had a moment when I just knew that book had to be written, isn't that odd? I'm an intuitive person, and I kind of wait for that "green light" feeling inside, then get to work.

Q: *Is there a particular character in* The Calder Game *that you identify with the most?*

A: It's hard to say . . . maybe Petra. I've been making mobile-poems, sometimes just in my imagination, since I was a teenager. And I understand Petra's way of doing things.

Q: *In* The Calder Game, *you introduce a controversial artist named Banksy. Why did you decide to weave him into the story?*

A: When I first stumbled on Banksy's art, in a newspaper article, I was so excited. He's both fearless and generous in the big questions he asks about art, and his ideas are so marvelously free. Plus, he's managed to protect his privacy — the public still doesn't know what he looks like. How cool is that?

Q: *While most of your characters are fictional, is it true that there's one particular four-legged character in* The Calder Game *who is in fact based on someone in your life?*

A: Absolutely. Our old cat, Pummie, is real — personality, shape, and all. He died just as I was finishing the book, at age 19. Everyone in the family misses him dreadfully.

Q: *Your books are popular with both boys and girls. Is that something you were trying to achieve?*

A: Yes. Having a son and daughters, and having taught school for many years, I knew a few secrets about the very real differences between boys and girls. And I don't mean stereotypical differences — just the ways in which they communicate and find meaning in the world around them. Knowing those secrets helped a lot.

Q: *Your previous books,* Chasing Vermeer *and* The Wright 3, *have codes embedded in the text and art. How did you develop the code in* The Calder Game?

A: Well, I came up with the codes in the text, for all three books, and Brett Helquist did the imaginative coding in the illustrations. The code in *The Calder Game* came right from Alexander Calder himself. It kind of jumped out at me one night as I lay in bed, studying photographs of his mobiles before going to sleep.

Q: *What have been your favorite responses to* Chasing Vermeer *and* The Wright 3?
A: Oh, I've received many, many fabulous letters from kids. I do love it when kids tell me that my books have changed the way they see their world, and made them believe that their ideas are important. Kids have told me that these books inspire them. That makes me so happy.

Q: *As a former teacher and now a full-time writer, what do you find more demanding and/or rewarding — teaching or writing?*
A: I loved teaching, it was very exciting and totally absorbing. And when I'm writing, I sometimes feel as though I'm still teaching — facilitating adventures, exploring ideas, learning as I go. It's great to believe so deeply in your lifework, and to be able to do it in a way that feels true. I am very lucky.

Q: *To what extent did your own childhood, growing up in New York City, influence your writing?*
A: At the time I grew up in New York, I think kids had more freedom to get around the city on their own. Museums were a good place to hang out, a place away from small apartments.

So the combination of independence and museums helped to form my way of seeing things, I'm sure.

Q: *You obviously spend a great deal of time developing, research-ing, and writing your stories. How do you spend your free time?*

A: My writing and my life aren't really that separate — things that I like to think about generally find their way into what I write. But I love to travel and read, and try to remember to notice the world around me: the shape of a puddle or a crack in the sidewalk, the light coming through a tulip in my kitchen, the beauty of an egg or a perfect apple.

Q: *Are you working on anything now?*

A: As soon as I finished *The Calder Game*, I found I was already sifting and stirring, thinking about possibilities for the next book. Yes, I'm currently researching, and the next book will have less art but more controversy. I love to make trouble of the right kinds!

Real Places, Real People

Calder Pillay, the character in Blue Balliett's *Chasing Vermeer*, *The Wright 3* and, of course, *The Calder Game*, is named after Alexander Calder, the American sculptor and artist whose mobiles and stabiles (as he liked to call them) are described in this book.

Alexander Calder was born on July 22, 1898, in Pennsylvania, and came from a long line of artists: his father, Alexander Stirling Calder, was a sculptor, and so was his grandfather, Alexander Milne Calder, who created the grand statue of William Penn on top of City Hall in Philadelphia.

Calder went to school to study mechanical engineering and worked as an engineer for a while, but he'd started creating small sculptures when he was young, and moved to New York City to study art. He eventually moved to Paris to pursue a career as an artist. There he married Louisa James (she was the grandniece of the author Henry James), and started to make toys and smaller sculptures out of various materials that could be moved. He created Cirque Calder, a miniature circus with puppets made of cloth, wire, and string that could be moved to "perform" the circus — you can see this moving sculpture today at the Whitney Museum of American Art in New York City.

In the 1930s, Alexander Calder was inspired by the abstract art of Joan Miró and Piet Mondrian, and decided to try to make abstract shapes (of painted metal and wires) move. These sculptures were hung from the ceiling, or balanced on stands — some were moved by motors, but others were pushed by the air. His friend Marcel Duchamp called them mobiles (Calder, Petra, and Tommy go to an exhibit of his mobiles on page 20). He also experimented with abstract sculptures that stood by themselves (like the Minotaur that Arthur Wish donates to Woodstock), which were called "stabiles" to differentiate them from the sculptures that moved. During World War II, when Calder couldn't get metal to work with, he created his sculptures out of carved wood.

Calder wasn't just a sculptor — he created jewelry and toys, he painted, and he even designed sets for the stage. He and his family settled into a home and studio in Connecticut, but Calder spent time in Paris as well as the United States. Alexander Calder passed away on November 11, 1976, but his work can still be seen all over the world. You can see *L'Homme* in Montreal, Canada; *La Spirale* in Paris, France; *El Sol Rojo* in Mexico City, Mexico; *Teodelapio* in Spoleto, Italy; and other pieces all over the United States (in New York City, Seattle, Washington DC, Honolulu, Chicago, and Houston to name a few cities).

Play the Calder Game!

On his trip to the Museum of Contemporary Art, Calder plays the Calder Game, and describes it to Petra and Tommy so they can play, too. There are examples of how to lay out a mobile design on page 34, but the sky is the limit! See if you can create a message, like Blue Balliett does in her dedication. What if you used your mobile to create a mood or feeling — could you use them as a journal entry like Petra does? What does this mobile make you think of?

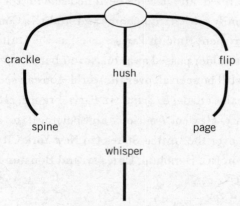

Now try getting your mobile off paper and into the air! Ms. Hussey's class was going to use found objects to play the Calder Game their way. Balance sea shells to remember a sunny day at the beach, hang pictures of your family to create a mobile family tree, use small things you can find or buy at a dollar store to make a mobile collage for a friend, or come up with a whole new idea of your own!

A Royal Forest

Woodstock is a real town in Oxfordshire, England. It's about eight miles away from Oxford, where you can find the oldest university in the English-speaking world. Woodstock has existed for a long time. King Alfred was supposed to have stayed there in the 800s, and King Henry II supposedly courted Fair Rosamund Clifford there during the 1100s (which probably threw Eleanor of Aquitaine into a queenly rage). Queen Mary I had her half sister imprisoned in the lodge at Woodstock in 1554 and 1555 after Wyatt's rebellion (she became Elizabeth I of England just a few years later).

In 1705, John Churchill, 1st Duke of Marlborough, was awarded for his successes as a general in the War of the Spanish Succession. Queen Anne gifted him with the manor of Woodstock and promised him funds to build a great palace there. Woodstock used to be a large manufacturer of gloves, and the poet Geoffrey Chaucer had a house there (which you can still see). Today the town attracts tourists to an amazing estate. Can you guess what it is?

Are you confused by all the Kings and Queens and Dukes? Titles of British nobility can be hard to keep track of, especially in countries where there isn't royalty. Though titles and rank can get terribly complicated (depending on whether a title can be passed to one's descendents, and who marries who), here's a very simple idea of how it works:

> Royalty:
> King/Queen (and their children)

Peerage:
Duke/Duchess
Marquess (or Marquis)/Marchioness
Earl/Countess
Viscount/Viscountess
Baron/Baroness

Gentry:
Baronet/Baronetess (or Baronet's wife if it's not
her title)
Knight/Lady (or Dame, or Knight's wife)
Scottish Baron/Scottish Baroness (or Scottish
Baron's wife)
Laird/Lady (or wife of a Laird)
Esquire
Gentleman

Did you guess why Woodstock doesn't depend on gloves any-more? One of the biggest draws to tourists in Woodstock is Blenheim Palace. This elaborate palace was begun in 1705 for John and Sarah Churchill, 1st Duke and Duchess of Marlborough. Blenheim Palace was modeled after the grand and stately palace at Versailles, France, and built in an elaborate baroque style — it was meant to be a monument to England. Sir John Vanbrugh designed the country house, and Capability Brown designed the landscaping for the grounds around the estate for the 4th Duke of Marlborough years later. The palace itself wasn't completed until after the first Duke had died, and Sarah finished it in 1725.

Does the name Churchill sound familiar? That might be because Sir Winston Churchill, the famous leader of the United Kingdom during World War II, was born in Blenheim Palace. He was the grandson of the 7th Duke of Marlborough, though he wasn't heir to the estate. Today Blenheim Palace is open to the public, though it's still the home of the 11th Duke of Marlborough and his family. Visitors can tour the palace and grounds like Calder did, or even hold conferences and weddings there. Scenes from the movies *The Scarlet Pimpernel*, *Indiana Jones and the Last Crusade*, and *Harry Potter and the Order of the Phoenix* were filmed at Blenheim Palace, too!

Play with an A-maze-ing Puzzle

"Penta" means "five" in Greek, and pentominoes are each made of five blocks. Can you guess how many blocks are in each of the octominoes? What about tetraminoes — have you ever played the video game Tetris?

Here's how to make your own set of pentominoes:

You'll need a pencil, a ruler, a highlighter or crayon, a 6" × 10" piece of thin cardboard (perhaps the cover of an old spiral notebook), and a pair of scissors.

1. Each of the twelve pentominoes in a set is made from 5 equal size squares. To make your set, begin by making a grid. Starting at a corner of your 6" × 10" piece of cardboard, make a tic-mark every inch along each edge of your rectangle.

2. Use your ruler and pencil to draw straight dark lines connecting the tic-marks top to bottom, then side to side, to create your grid.

3. Following the diagram below, outline each five-square pentomino with your highlighter or crayon.

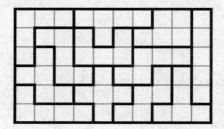

4. Now you're ready to cut out your pentominoes. Cut straight along the highlighted lines.

Try this: Calder is inspired by the maze at Blenheim Palace, and he starts using his pentominoes to create mazes on graph paper. You can try this yourself after you've made a set — try different combinations of pentominoes, or different sizes of space to work on. There are a couple examples of Calder's mazes on pages 99 and 100. What else can you come up with? What could you do with two or more sets of pentominoes?

Designated Graffiti Area

Banksy. No one really knows who he (or she? or they?) is, other than a street artist probably born in 1974 in Bristol, England. He started as a graffiti artist in the early 1990s, and found that he was coming close to getting caught, or taking too long to finish his work. Since graffiti is considered vandalism in many countries, he needed to speed things up, and began using stencils that were made before going out to spray paint his art so that he could create pieces faster. Banksy has created art all over the world, and is known for art that contains strong social or political commentary — his signs that say plain walls are official graffiti areas, or painting "this is not a photo opportunity" in picturesque spots highlight how little people pay attention to the world around them, and how little they think about what they're reading.

A lot of what Banksy does — graffiti in public places, hanging up his own art in museums — is illegal, but you can still take his message to heart like Art Wish does with his WISH stencil. Be on the lookout for new ways to define art. Maybe there's a statue in your town that you've seen hundreds of times — have you ever looked at it closely? Do you know what it's of, or why it's there, or who made it?

If you can print out or find a poster or postcard of a famous painting, you can make art like Banksy does. He once used a reproduction of one of Monet's water lily paintings and added shopping carts sinking into the pond amongst the lilies. Find a piece that speaks to you, or that you don't like or